GRAHAM LIRONI is a son and a brother
and a husband and a father. He's a lover,
not a fighter. An award-winning journalist,
he currently edits two of Scotland's leading
business magazines and is a founder member of
the avant-punk beat combo The Secret Goldfish.

Graham lives and works in Glasgow.

The Bowels of Christ is his first novel.

For Margaret,
best wishes and Merry Christmas!

9.12.96

The Bowels of Christ

a first novel by

Graham Lironi

BLACK ACE BOOKS

First published in 1996 by Black Ace Books
Ellemford, Duns, TD11 3SG, Scotland

© Graham Lironi 1996

Typeset by Black Ace Editorial
Ellemford, Duns, TD11 3SG, Scotland

Printed in England by Redwood Books
Kennet House, Kennet Way, Trowbridge, BA14 8RN

A CIP catalogue record for this book
is available from the British Library

ISBN   1–872988–71–7

The publishers gratefully acknowledge
subsidy from the Scottish Arts Council
towards the production of this first edition

ACKNOWLEDGEMENTS

The author would like to thank
Peter Gilmour, Iain Beveridge, Ian Lister,
Alison McBride, Clive Peebles and Ann Donald
for their assistance.

The publishers are grateful to
Douglas Dunn, for permission to quote
from his poem 'Art Is Wonderful'
and to the *Herald* for permission
to quote from contemporary reports
in the *Glasgow Herald*.

'Tis strange – but true; for truth is always strange;
Stranger than fiction.

Lord Byron

For Allison,

All love lasts
if something occurs naturally.

This is a true story.

Part I

THE REAL THING

They say that in the wood
you get what nearly everybody here
is longing for – a second chance.

J.M. Barrie

1a

A Cold Rage

On the eve of Halloween 1969, twenty-four-year-old James Nelson battered his mother to death in the family home in Garrowhill, Lanarkshire, in what was referred to at his trial as 'a cold rage'.

Immediately prior to the brutal murder, he had returned home from a date with his girlfriend while his father and sister were at choir practice. A row developed between Nelson and his mother, culminating in him beating her to the ground with a truncheon and brick.

Fourteen years later the *Glasgow Herald* reported Nelson as recounting to journalist Stewart Lamont that, as he struck, a demonic rage seemed to grow and a few moments later he regained his senses, realizing there was a brick in his hand which he could not remember using.

His mother lay dying at his feet.

At that moment, Nelson was to tell Lamont, he felt no horror at what he had done. It was, he said, as if an outside force were motivating him. He then hid his mother's body in the garage, washed, changed his clothes and fled.

It was then that a voice of conscience whispered in his ear:

'Why are you running away?'

He returned home and confessed to police who had already arrived at the scene of the crime.

James Nelson was convicted in 1970 of murdering his mother.

16

Sunday Afternoon

It was a dreich Sunday afternoon.

Drizzle dampened the spirit of the city's long-suffering citizens. The city was Glasgow; a city used to being rained on. An outside observer might have proposed that the inhabitants of such a raindrained metropolis must have grown to accept their precipitative fate. Such a proposition would be mistaken.

Glaswegians loathe rain.

They distribute this loathing amongst themselves according to the same egalitarian principles upon which their political sensibilities are founded. That is, they *im*plicitly despise the few with sufficient wealth to soak up excessive quantities of loathing and *ex*plicitly sympathize with the toiling masses, seeking to ensure that the loathing is shared equally amongst as large a percentage of the population as possible.

If socialism is a system whereby the means of producing and distributing goods are owned collectively and political power is exercised by the whole community, then Glasgow is a city of socialists – insofar as an essential ingredient of the philosophy of its citizenship is faith in the tenets of socialism. It is this aspect of themselves which they consider sets them apart from their neighbours south of the border, whom they despise, and in the capital of their own nation only forty miles to the east (yet across a great cultural chasm), whom they also despise. At least some of this despising can be attributed to the fact that neither England nor Edinburgh is perceived to suffer from the same level of rainfall as Glasgow.

It was a dreich Sunday afternoon of the kind when the inhabitants of the city's west end stay resolutely behind closed doors to scrutinize Sunday supplements prior to venturing out to gossip about current affairs. It is an easy and futile existence, reflected in the fact that the word *existence* does not appear in their vocabulary, having been replaced by the less offensive *lifestyle*. Such subtle changes in language help soothe the perplexity experienced by those with sufficient perception to recognize the essential futility of their existence but without the imagination required to effect an alternative.

The east end of Glasgow is an altogether different terrain. It is there that the couple necessary for this story to begin are to be found.

1c

Day-trippers

The existence of inhabitants in the east end of Glasgow is no less futile than that of their west end counterparts, but their lack of style results in their substitute for the word *existence* being the equally bleak *life*. There is not much comfort for the eastender mulling over the futility of his *life*.

It was in the east end of Glasgow, on a dreich Sunday afternoon, that a couple stepped out of Spoutmouth and walked in synchronization towards the Barras.

On Sunday afternoons the Barras is a popular location with bargain hunters who browse around grimy stalls of books, records and other assorted ephemera. The bargain hunters may be eastenders, westenders, southsiders or day-trippers who have travelled into the city centre from the surrounding environs to rummage listlessly around. The aforementioned couple belonged in the latter category.

The fact that they were not native eastenders could be deduced from their incongruous appearance. They had in fact commuted into the city centre from East Kilbride, a location which prides itself on being Scotland's oldest new town. Such towns, of which there are five, are identical Legoland localities consisting of large blocks of roughcast houses, each block having its own square of shops, with one large town centre where more shops, public houses and local government offices are located. The blocks are connected to the town centre and to neighbouring blocks via an extensive network of dual carriageways and roundabouts.

The couple who were strolling around the Barras on this particular dreich Sunday afternoon lived in the same cul-de-sac in East Kilbride.

They marched heroically through the bustling crowd. They passed traders displaying curtain material, rattling off discounts at such a rapid rate and in such a thick tongue that none but the native eastender could comprehend what was on offer and at what price. As they marched through this cacophony they collected fragmentary impressions about the nature of the place which, when assimilated, formed a prosaic mosaic.

It was, they surmised, a place peopled by poor, foul-mouthed, disease-ridden child smokers and no-hopers with primitively self-tattooed forearms and snot-nosed infant cherubs shouting *Fuck this* and *Fuck that*, who stank of BO and had lank lice-ridden hair, chewed fingers, scarred cheeks, squint eyes, harelips and halitosis, and who wore milk-bottle NHS specs, second-hand ill-fitting clothes, navy snorkels with Sellotaped slashes, lime V-necks without shirts but brown cord bell-bottoms, unlaced shoes, laddered tights and dirty, wrinkled, unmatched socks.

They marched past stalls selling lingerie, overcoats, candyfloss, cheap radios and watches, second-hand furniture and broken bric-a-brac. Simultaneously, and independently of each other, they arrived at the conclusion that the items were a reflection of the crowd, and vice versa.

As they marched, their incongruous appearance set them

apart from the crowd and yielded a greater number of doubletakes than might reasonably have been anticipated.

The incongruousness of the pair was compounded *because* they were a pair, the appearance of the first being simultaneously strikingly similar to, and totally opposite to, that of the second. They appeared to be of identical height and build. Both marched with shoulders hunched against the rain, heads hung low with fists thrust deep into pockets. Both wore clothes identical except for colour. One was dressed entirely in white, with a black cap; the other entirely in black, with a white cap.

The effect was that one looked like a negative, or positive, image of the other.

It was not only the striking similarity of the couple or the combined visual impact of the clothes they chose to wear that intrigued onlookers; it was the fact that the absence of any obvious sign of masculinity or femininity introduced scope for conjecture into the normally instinctive process of gender identification.

Those passers-by with an eye for detail, though, noticed a minor but crucial difference. While their faces bore a remarkably androgynous resemblance, a thick black slug arched over each eye of the white-capped one. Slugs were conspicuous by their absence from the brow of the black-capped other. This difference was considered sufficient evidence, by those onlookers who noticed it, to classify the slug-eyed one as male and the other as female.

The pair of day-trippers came to a halt before a black ramshackle caravan and read a sign dangling from its door handle. In flowery green hand-painted letters which had started to run with the rain, on a bile-yellow background, a cardboard sign bore the hand-scrawled words:

Madame Selene

Palmist

Have palm read for £5

1d

Fire and Earth

It was dark inside the caravan because the windows had been painted black. While the pair's eyes sought to adjust to a dim, candle-lit interior, their nostrils were hit by a heady brew of pot pourri and incense. Soon they saw that they stood in a cluttered, confined space crammed with odd items of furniture and countless shaky columns of books which stretched from the floor to the arched ceiling, their musty pages contributing to the stuffy atmosphere.

Behind a small, unstable table, upon which rested a crystal ball and scattered tarot cards, sat a gypsy, scrunched up and peering from watery eyes at an enormous antiquarian encyclopaedia. A jade robe shrouded all but her dark Romany face and hands. She glanced up, only now aware of their presence, and scrutinized them. Madame Selene had an unsightly wart on her left cheek from which a cluster of long black hairs sprouted. Large gold-hooped stereotypical earrings swung from her surprised jerk.

She beckoned them.

The black-capped one sat in a chair opposite, the white-capped other stood close behind.

'Five pounds,' said the gypsy. Her voice was husky and Mediterranean.

The seated one fumbled in a pocket and extracted a crisp, new Autobank blue.

Madame Selene accepted it with a withered hand. 'What's your name?' she croaked.

'Carol.'

The gypsy proceeded to quiz Carol about her age, nationality, medical history and whether she was left- or right-handed.

Carol replied that she was sixteen, Scottish, healthy and right-handed.

The gypsy then asked to see her hands. 'Your right hand tells me *what* you are,' she said in a low, slow tone, 'your left, what you *could be*.' The old woman contemplated the young, firm-fleshed hands, running her bony fingers along Carol's palm lines. Then she sat back and sighed through clasped hands.

A candle shivered.

'You've a Fire Hand,' she began, 'a rectangular palm with short fingers. You're restless. Your assertiveness means you take the lead where the opposite sex is concerned. You can be selfish and aggressive, particularly in your dealings with the slower and more cautious Earth and Water types. Your life line appears straightforward, except for a small break at the start.'

'What does that mean?' interrupted Carol.

'Maybe nothing, but it could mean that you're in danger. You have a fleshy mount under your ring finger, which indicates vanity.'

Carol shrugged. 'The ugly're always the most vain,' she said. But Carol was not ugly and nor did she consider herself to be so. Neither did she consider herself vain. She had long since concluded that vanity is a trait more common in the male.

Madame Selene sighed through the cathedral she had formed with her hands, and closed her eyes. When she opened them again she sensed that something was different but was unable to specify precisely what. Then she noticed that her reclining client wore a white cap while the erect other's was black. Pipping her request for further remuneration, five single pound notes were swiftly fanned out on the table before her. Unperturbed, the gypsy proceeded to pose the same series of questions she had asked Carol.

Excepting the answers given to her first and last queries, the responses received were identical. The exceptions were that her second client's name was given as Carl, who revealed that he was left-handed.

'For you it is the opposite of Carol,' said the gypsy. 'Your *left* hand shows what you are, your *right* what you could be.' After poring over the pattern of his palms, she sat back to deliver her verdict:

'You've a square palm with short fingers,' she began. 'That's an Earth Hand. You prefer to go with the flow rather than swim against it. You're honest, with lots of common sense. Your head line has a distinct fork and branches towards Luna. These suggest that you may lie. You've a small break in your heart line which could show something serious, such as the end of a long affair or the death of someone you love.'

With that, Madame Selene closed her eyes and, covering her face with her hands, sighed deeply. Then she whispered:

Mother ice and daughter water
will bring you tears of sorrow and joy.
Time will burn you, then return you
to tomorrow's miracle boy.

2a

Mountains

There's something sublime about standing at the top of a mountain; it's a consequence of the combination of an unknown quantity of factors. Partly it's a consequence of the amount of energy exerted in scaling a mountain and the sense of achievement experienced on eventually reaching its summit. That is,

$$s = e + a,$$

where s represents sublimity, e represents energy and a represents sense of achievement.

Such a simple equation is supported by the appealing theory that someone who scales the mountain through his or her own endeavours is rewarded with a greater sense of achievement and experiences a greater sense of sublimity than one who has taken a chairlift to the summit. In other words, the greater the value of e, the greater the value of a and, consequently, the greater the value of s. But there is more to sublimity than just energy exerted plus a sense of achievement.

Partly it's a consequence of the pervading silence which,

due to its abstraction from twentieth-century existence and mysterious eternal quality, brings the reality of the ephemeral nature of the human entity sharply into focus. This is because, having robbed us of two of the three principal opiums of the people – television and music – silence reawakens the capacity for realizing the potential implicit in the very condition of being alive lying dormant within each of us.

Partly, too, it's a consequence of the beauty of the panorama afforded by such an elevated position. The contemplation of a natural landscape from such a vantage point is a study in exaltation. The solidity and perpetuity of mountains accentuates the awareness of our own transience.

Such is the awesome power of their permanence that, when standing on top of a mountain, it may occur to the climber that, had another climber stood in the same position one hundred years earlier, contemplating the same beautiful panorama, the same metaphysical thoughts might well have occurred to *that* climber: contemplating the possibility of another climber standing on top of a mountain contemplating the same beautiful panorama a hundred years before *him*. If the years are counted in thousands rather than hundreds, and if we recognize that they can go forwards as well as backwards, then the implications of such contemplation become all the more apparent.

And so the original, deceptively simple, definition of sublimity has become more complex. A new equation may be illustrated as:

$$s = e + a + si + bp + x,$$

where s represents sublimity, e represents energy, a represents sense of achievement, si represents silence, bp represents the beauty of the panorama and x represents the unknown number of other factors.

But the combination of such factors has a synergistic effect which makes the mathematics more complex still.

2b

The First Intoxication

The mathematical complexities of sublimity didn't interest Carol or Carl, but the sense of sublimity experienced when standing on top of a mountain did. It was a sensation which they'd shared on numerous occasions, though the satisfactory communication of it had always eluded them. The sensation rendered them inarticulate, an affliction common to such circumstances, but it was a sensation to which, after their first intoxication, they had become addicted.

The first intoxication had occurred on a hot May day three years previously. On an end-of-term school trip to Rowardennan on the banks of Loch Lomond, a class of thirty thirteen-year-olds embarked on an ascent to the summit of Ben Lomond. Two of the thirty were Carol and Carl. The first two to reach the summit, and the last two to descend from it, were Carol and Carl.

They returned to Rowardennan exhilarated in their exhaustion. As they entered the school bus to travel home to East Kilbride, Carl noticed that the seat of Carol's jeans was stained with blood. Concerned for her welfare, he asked if she had injured herself. Carol's dismissive response to his enquiry, and her obstinate refusal to elucidate, troubled him.

The fact was that the Carol and Carl who had returned to the foot of Ben Lomond were different to the Carol and Carl who had set off to reach its summit five hours earlier. They were different because they'd discovered the sublimity of standing on top of a mountain. Carol was different in an additional, more physical, sense. She had set off from the foot of Ben Lomond a girl, and returned from its summit a woman.

2c

The Pilgrimage

The Ben Lomond excursion was the first of many day trips to Loch Lomond and the Arrochar Alps made by the pair that summer. The following Saturday they climbed the Cobbler and the Saturday after that Ben Vane. They often sought to satisfy their craving for exhaustion by rambling throughout East Kilbride's Calderglen on midweek evenings, but the terrain did not sufficiently test their strength and resulted more in frustration than exaltation.

The following summer the ambitious duo embarked on the West Highland Way, departing from Milngavie early one Saturday and arriving at Fort William late on the following Tuesday. On the Wednesday they scaled Ben Nevis. An observer might have predicted that it would not be too long before they progressed to mountaineering, which would seem to offer the attraction of a greater sense of achievement due to the addition of an element of danger, and the high level of skill required, to the considerable stamina necessary for hillwalking.

Such a prediction would be misplaced.

Although the pair would not deny these attractions, the element of danger intrinsic to mountaineering discouraged them from further progression. While both shared a tendency towards timidity, they were equally well endowed with common sense. This ensured that they remained on the safe side of the boundary between mountaineering and hillwalking. Common sense meant they were invariably well prepared for each of their excursions, having allocated sufficient time to plan their proposed route with a diligence unusual in two so young.

It was a quality upon which they were to draw extensively the following summer during a six-week Munro-bagging holiday. On their return from this ambitious expedition, their satisfaction from having conquered the remaining highest mountains in Scotland was tinged with a pinch of chagrin at having done just that.

This chagrin soon metamorphosed into anticipation at the prospect of exploring virgin territory. Neither Carol nor Carl had ever ventured beyond the boundaries of their native country, nor had it occurred to them to do so. But the independence and tacit approval the two had earned as a consequence of their self-evident maturity, to which a catalogue of challenging expeditions devoid of incident stood testament, meant that, at the tender age of sixteen, they could now consider the opportunity of a world of adventure packed with spectacular perspectives.

The sweetness of the anticipation, born of the prospect of embarking on a pilgrimage to the earth's most beautiful natural legacies, was of such potency that it nourished their desire for new peaks of sublimity for a whole year. Such a pilgrimage would, after all, require meticulous planning.

The first and most important decision concerned location. After detailed discussion, the two opted for Macchu Picchu, an Aztec mountain in Peru. Carol had seen a colour photograph of it in a glossy Sunday supplement and the image had revealed a world of wild wonder lying outwith the limits of her own home-grown imagination. She cut the photograph from the magazine and pinned it above her bed. This was torn from the wall, crumpled into a ball and hurled in the direction of a bin lurking in a corner of her room when her discovery of the reality of economics placed Macchu Picchu firmly within the realms of fantasy.

The photograph which replaced it could not have been more different.

Except for a small blue triangle pointing down from the centre of its top edge, it was entirely blank. Closer inspection revealed a landscape of snow, with the blue triangle a portion of sky visible between neighbouring giants. This was a view of the Alps shot from the Val d'Ayas valley.

It was with the goal of becoming two specks lost within the vast white void of this very image that Carol and Carl passed a year in preparation. They carried out extensive research into the articles of clothing required and any additional climbing equipment necessary. Purchasing forays were made into Glasgow. It was the last of these, when Carol treated Carl to a present of a Swiss Army knife bought from a surplus store on the edge of the Barras, which led to their encounter with Madame Selene.

A week later, two specks trudged into the blank landscape, just above the photograph's lower edge.

2d

The Reverie

The snow was deep and crisp. The sky was cloudless and blue. The sun caught the crystals of condensation which shot from their mouths like dragons' breath at frequent, regular intervals. The scale of the landscape dwarfed their naive dogmatism.

They had departed four hours earlier from Champoluc, an Italian resort in the Val d'Ayas valley at the foot of the Alps, with the intention of crossing the border with Switzerland. The route they had mapped out led them between the twin peaks of Castor and Pollux, around Mont Blanc, along a narrow pass and down a glacier into Switzerland.

They had already learned to their cost that planning is no substitute for experience. While the presence of snow had been anticipated in theory, their inexperience of ploughing through it meant that, in the calculation of their schedule, they had neglected to allow for the degree of exhaustion they now experienced. It had taken them four hours to reach the point they had expected to reach in two.

Since they had initially calculated the journey would take ten hours to complete, at their current pace the revised duration from departure to arrival was doubled to twenty hours. This revision had an important implication; it meant that, because they had set forth at 10 a.m. and the sky started to darken at 8 p.m., they would need to endure the night on the mountain.

It was a tribute to their fastidiousness that they had prepared for just this eventuality. Though they had camped out overnight on the odd occasion before, when circumstances had necessitated they do so, it was not an experience which either relished. The combination of silence, darkness and homeless loneliness resulted in a sense of vulnerability. This vulnerability encouraged insomnia which, in turn, compounded the vulnerability. The result was a strained vigilance overfed by two overactive imaginations. But since the thought of returning to base did not occur to them, they accepted their fate.

The revised goal for the day was to cover as much ground as possible before eight o'clock.

At the appointed hour, the exhausted twosome slipped free from their cumbersome rucksacks, lay spreadeagled against the quilt of snow and let the sky of unblemished blue soothe their aching muscles. They had managed to reach further than the halfway stage their revised calculations had predicted. Castor and Pollux now lay behind them and, according to Carol's compass, they were well on their way around Mont Blanc.

They had reached the high point, in terms of altitude, of their journey. The relief was almost palpable.

It took great willpower to rise from the comfort of the snow-quilt and set up camp, but when they did they worked methodically and in silence. It was dark by the time the small tent was erect. Lack of appetite and surplus of fatigue eclipsed the need for sustenance and so, by consent, they prepared for sleep. But Carol's sense of vulnerability had heightened with the fading light. Although exhausted, she was unable to slow her thoughts down sufficiently to sink into the sleep so craved by her body.

She began to feel claustrophobic.

Her thoughts raced through the events of the day. It occurred to her that the day before she had been in East Kilbride. This struck her as incredible. Yesterday belonged to a previous, secure existence. She now inhabited a strange world where people spoke a language she could not comprehend.

The effect of this novelty was exciting and disconcerting; like a narcotic which gave her a sudden rush of euphoria, but with a disproportionate degree of paranoid angst as a side effect. East Kilbride had become a drab abstraction. She had entered a new phase and the mundanity of her previous life now seemed a waste of precious time.

The side effect left her with a sense that, by accepting her roughcast suburban fate as given, she had missed the opportunity to force back the frontiers of potential experience, but the burst of euphoria allowed her a glimpse at the enormity of the world and its myriad possibilities. Inspired, she realized that her only limitation was imagination. Simultaneously, and schizophrenically, she longed for the secure, suburban sanity of East Kilbride. Eventually Carol's tortured psyche attained such a velocity and her claustrophobia such intensity that she conceded defeat to insomnia and thrust her head outside the confines of the tent.

What she beheld was the most beautiful spectacle she had ever witnessed. A full moon hung in a starry sky casting a blue tone over a landscape of sparkling snow. The air was still. The mountains slept. Carol *absorbed* the silence. Motionless, she observed the splendour, transfixed by its ethereal magnificence till tears blurred her vision. Her ruminations ground to a halt. When she awoke from this reverie she was calm. With her sensibility returned to normality, she became newly aware of the sub-zero temperature. The cold seeped speedily into her marrow. Zipping the tent shut, she curled into the foetal position and began to rock gently. When sleep still refused to descend, she began to whimper.

'You okay?' asked Carl.

His voice took her by surprise. It came from a reality outwith her own temporarily narrowed field of perception, plucking her from internal turmoil and placing her firmly back into a shared, external context. She was grateful for it.

'Freezing,' she replied.

'Me too.'

Sleep had also denied Carl its therapy. He had lain awake as long as Carol. His introspection had hurtled along parallel tracks to hers.

'I can't sleep,' said Carol.

'Me neither.'

'I'm scared.'

Carl shuffled closer and stretched his arm over Carol's shoulder.

'We should share our body heat,' he whispered.

2e

The Significance of Touch

That night Carol and Carl learned the significance of touch.

Sexual intercourse is a potent act, particularly when performed by two sixteen-year-old virgins in love. Love is a potent concept, particularly when permitted to flourish between a romantic pair of sixteen-year-old virgins.

That night Carol and Carl's love for each other progressed to a point beyond conception to became the reality in relation to which the otherwise absurdity of their lives revolved. The catalyst of this radical progression was the introduction of the sexual element to their hitherto platonic love. Coition swept them to a climax which miniaturised the sublimity felt when standing on top of a mountain. Hillwalking had been stripped of its majesty and replaced by an experience which truly fused flesh and spirit to create a real thing beyond fantasy.

2f

Three Minutes of Honesty

Carol was the first to wake.

She was immediately made aware of the cold and the fundamental change in the nature of her relationship with Carl. Shivering, she rolled from beneath his sprawling arm, lightly kissed his forehead and dressed as quietly as she could.

Her conscience troubled her. Carl, she reasoned, would reassure her when he awoke.

Clothed, Carol crawled outside the tent. A bitter breeze blew into her. She screwed up her eyes. It seemed an entirely different landscape from that which she had felt so privileged to witness the previous evening. The snow dazzled with sharp intensity and the blue mellow mountains of yesterday's dusk had developed into the harsh focus of reality, softened only by a low coverlet of woolly mist.

The sound of movement meant Carl had woken.

Carol returned inside the tent.

'What time's it?' he asked, stretching and yawning.

These were not the words she had anticipated.

'Time to get up,' she answered, already packing things neatly away. 'There's mist falling.'

It seemed odd to her that he made no reference to their mutual loss of virginity and discovery of ecstasy the night before. She reasoned that perhaps he was embarrassed or perhaps he too nursed a nagging sense of guilt. Whatever the reason, they seemed unable to articulate the significant new twist in their relationship and attempted, instead, to pretend it was unchanged.

It was still steering a course into uncharted territory five hours later. During that time they had threaded their way around black crevasses and crossed snow bridges over chasms of ice, yet barely a word had passed between them. The mist had surreptitiously enveloped them in a thick cloud. They proceeded with caution. Removing a rope from his rucksack, Carl tied one end tightly around his waist and recommended to Carol that she do the same with the other. This she did when he explained that the poor visibility necessitated such a precaution. This was true. It was also true that their bond had eroded to such an extent that this rope was now all that held them together; or so it seemed to Carol.

Silence breathed life into the dubiety which now shrouded her like the mist shrouded the sun. The most beautifully profound experience, the final conjugation of twin souls which had yearned for each other throughout eternity, had been nothing more than a figment of her imagination. This was a notion she was unable to accept without his confirmation. Until that morning Carol had never doubted Carl's love for her. Now there remained nothing but doubt.

When she could bear the burden of silence no longer, she said:

'Carl, be honest with me—'

'Listen,' he interrupted, 'show me someone who's honest

and I'll show you someone who's very lonely. *No* relationship between two people could survive if they were honest with each other.'

Carol stopped dead. When he ran out of rope, Carl stopped too. She was astonished by the violence of this outburst. When she had pondered its content, she asked:

'So you lie to me?'

When this met with an immediate affirmation, she was plunged into an inferno of confusion. The unflinching callousness of his reply made a nonsense of all she felt she had known to be true. The boy with whom she had nurtured her love for as long as she could remember despised her when that love found its supreme expression.

An idea occurred to her; a test by which she would defy his cynicism. 'All right,' she said, 'let's see if our relationship can survive three minutes of honesty.'

GOVERNMENT HEALTH WARNING:
HONESTY CAN SERIOUSLY DAMAGE YOUR HEALTH

'Are you serious?'

'Deadly.'

'I don't think it's a good idea.'

'Why not?'

'Someone might get hurt.'

Moving closer, Carol searched his eyes for what she thought she had once seen there.

'I don't understand you,' she said, shaking her head. 'You're trying to tell me that *three minutes* of honesty could ruin our relationship? Is the *whole thing* based on lies?'

'Not exactly lies,' he admitted. 'Not deliberate, malicious

42

lies, anyway. But white lies, misconceptions; misinterpret-ations. Not telling the whole truth, untold secrets, fact distortion—'

'All right,' interrupted Carol. 'Let's see if we can survive three minutes then, okay?'

Carl shrugged and sighed:

'Okay, but I don't think it's a good idea.'

She removed her watch and held it where they could both see its face. As the second hand jerked to twelve, Carol said:

'Three minutes of honesty starting . . . *now!*'

Carl yawned. 'Come on then,' he taunted.

'Are you happy?'

'No.'

'Why not?'

'Don't know.'

'What d'you . . . think of me?'

'What d'you mean?'

'Do you . . . love me?'

Although her voice begged him to say yes, Carl made no indication that he had heard her.

She waited. 'Do you—'

'I . . . don't know,' he said, cutting her off.

Carol was dumbfounded.

'I don't know if I even *believe* in love,' continued Carl, seemingly oblivious to the repercussions of his viciousness. 'I'm not certain it exists.'

Carol turned away.

'That's only a minute and already we're on shaky ground,' said Carl. 'I told you it was a bad—'

Carol was running, screaming her torment. The rope jolted, catching Carl off guard, but the strength of her momentum carried him in tow and suddenly there was a second scream, different to the first though emanating from the same mouth. The difference was that the first was a scream of sorrow while the second was of terror.

Carol had fallen over a cliff.

Carl was yanked violently to a ground of solid ice and dragged to the edge of the precipice. He came to rest jack-knifed over the cliff-face. The combined weight of himself, Carol and their rucksacks pulled down on his trembling elbows. As he fought desperately to maintain a shaky equilibrium, Carol dangled on the end of a string, a whimpering puppet.

'Try not to move!' he shouted.

In a moment, it occurred to him what to do; it took him a moment longer to conclude he had no other option. Slowly and methodically, he removed from the breast pocket of his shirt the Swiss Army knife Carol had bought him a week earlier, opened out the largest blade and sawed at the rope beneath his waist.

Seconds later Carl's burden became significantly lighter and Carol released a third and final scream of such shattering magnitude that it was able to reach up, grab a hold of Carl's guts and drag them down to share the sweetness of his reason. Cautiously, Carl managed to lever himself up to safety. Lying there on his back, panting, he could still hear her scream piercing his peace, fading towards silence though never falling silent, destined to forever reverberate within the space vacated by his guts.

He peered over the precipice but his vision was obscured by a thick cloud of mist.

3a

The Ritual

Fifers are a different breed to the west-coast Scot. Their lilting, earthy tongue is as hard on the ear to the Glaswegian as the Glaswegian's ugly brogue is to the rest of Britain.

Predominantly a rural region, Fife is home to decent folk whose stoicism is a reflection of the quiet acceptance of all the bleak elements nature can throw at them. At an early age the oppressive influence of the Kirk deprives the young Fifer of joy and replaces it with sensibleness. At a later stage it drives the older Fifer to drink, to dull the dangerous notion that a Calvinistic existence is a dead excuse for a life.

Alice McIntyre was a young Fifer.

At the age of ten she was a slip of a girl, the smallest and skinniest in her class, with long mousey hair which her mother put in pigtails tied with rubber bands. She was not pretty and she was not plain. She had the kind of face which gets lost in a crowd.

Alice was the kind of girl who liked to get lost in a crowd; not because of the bustle a throng might offer, but because of the opportunity for anonymity and escape from the scrutiny of the Great Unblinking Eye which stared down and noted everything she said and did.

Alice spoke in a barely audible whisper. Neighbours considered her someone who 'liked to keep herself to herself', but they were missing the point entirely. As far as Alice was concerned, her shyness lay outwith her control. It was at the age of ten that she developed the symptom of her shyness which would forever plague her.

One day her teacher, a tight-lipped spinster who scraped and strangled her hair into a severe bun, ordered her to read a passage from the Bible to the rest of the class. Alice began slowly and shakily, reciting Christ's crucifixion in her delicate manner – when the teacher thundered:

'Speak *up* girl!' and slammed a Bible down on her desk with such violence that the fright she gave the poor girl was made instantly tangible by the birth of an incurable stutter.

Alice was the only child of dutiful parents.

Her mother and father were typical of Fife parents in that, whilst they loved their daughter dearly, they were incapable of expressing this to her. Mr and Mrs McIntyre would go out of their way to hide any explicit evidence of their love *for* her *from* her, on the assumption that it was an accepted truth lying beyond the necessity of articulation. Consequently, Alice grew up without the comfort of certainty.

On the surface her parents reacted to the emergence of her stutter with understanding diplomacy, reassuring themselves that it was nothing more than an indication of temporary trauma. Beneath this veneer seethed mystified impatience with their only child's lack of self-esteem. Alice's sensitivity meant that she could see through her parent's sympathy to the resentment underlying it.

Her parents were upstanding members of the close-knit community of Cupar who revelled in active participation in local affairs. Her father was a prominent member of the Scottish National Party's local branch and her mother was a proud housewife who derived a comforting glow of goodness from the leading role she played in the kirk choir each Sunday.

Alice and her parents attended the kirk with religious regularity. In her father's case, out of a sense of duty to, and respect for, the establishment; in her mother's, out of unswerving faith in the beliefs of the Presbyterian Church of Scotland and, in Alice's own case, because she had no choice in the matter. It never occurred to her to question the authority of her parents.

Weekday evenings in the McIntyre household were endured in respectful silence. Her moustachioed bald father slumped into his armchair, which sat in prime position before a blazing hearth, placed his slippered feet atop a pouffe and, sucking on a pipe, read the *Courier*. After Alice and her mother had washed, dried and put away the pots, pans, plates and cutlery into their respective cupboards and drawers, the bespectacled Mrs McIntyre joined her husband in the living room where she scanned *People's Friend* and knitted her spouse an item of clothing such as the beige cardigan she had made for him well over a decade ago and which he still wore to this day.

Alice, meanwhile, retired to her bedroom after tea to do her homework before burying her head in a library book.

A grandfather clock marked off the sluggish, silent hours with monotonous regularity. When it chimed nine times, Alice would descend the stairs, enter the living room and, pecking her parents once each on the cheek, bid them good night.

It was a ritual devoid of emotion. It was a ritual performed *because* it was a ritual.

36

A Red Bandana

Six years later, when Alice was halfway through her fourth year at secondary school, she had an encounter with a boy which nudged the rudder of her destiny from steering a course towards calm seas and clear skies into troubled waters with hidden depths.

They met at a party, the first and last of its kind Alice was ever to attend. The hostess was a classmate called Kirsty who had just turned sixteen. Alice accepted her invitation to attend after seeking and receiving parental approval. The evening proved to be revelational.

That night she was, inadvertently, introduced to alcohol; inadvertently, because she did not knowingly accept a drink. Kirsty, she had supposed, had been the perfect hostess by ensuring that she was delivered with a constant supply of Coke. It was not until some days later that Alice realized her Coke had been laced with vodka.

Shortly after eleven o'clock the party was gatecrashed by a gang of bikers from the nearby village of Ladybank. Before this intrusion could erupt into violence, Kirsty quickly and sensibly declared that the gatecrashers were welcome.

Clad in black leathers, the five-strong gang passed a bottle of El Dorado amongst their number and smoked roll-ups. Their style seemed to impress the fourth-year nymphs, for it was not long before four of the five had a giggling girl dangling from each arm.

Alice was not one of them.

As the bikers had made their dramatic entrance, she had slipped from the room. Suffering from a strange sickness, she ran upstairs to the bathroom and vomited.

When someone on the other side of the door threatened to kick it down unless it was opened by the time he had counted to three, she hauled herself on to unsteady legs. The moment she unlocked the latch two boys barged in and she was unceremoniously shoved into the landing.

She stood swaying at the head of the stairs, holding the banister for support. At first she was too busy fighting for breath to realize that she was barring the way of the fifth biker, who stood a couple of stairs below. Except for a red bandana, he was clothed entirely in shiny black leather.

Alice noticed that his lips were moving.

'P-P-P-P-Pardon?' she stammered.

Then the two boys who had ejected her from the toilet shoved past. Losing her grip on the banister, Alice began to reel. Giddy, her vision clouded. If the biker had not been there she would have fallen headfirst down the stairs. But he *was* there. He caught her and carried her into the fresh night air. When she regained consciousness, Alice found herself lying on Kirsty's doorstep, her head cradled in the arms of the biker who crouched over her, dabbing her fevered brow with a moist bandana.

'You okay?' he asked.

She nodded.

'I'll run you home.'

She started to protest but was silenced when he put a finger to his lips.

3c

Monday Morning

At school it seemed to Alice that Kirsty was behaving very sheepishly. Then, at lunchtime, an odd thing happened. Two boys approached her in the playground, both nursing black eyes. With hangdog expressions, they asked her to accept their apologies. Later she recognized them as the two who had ejected her from Kirsty's toilet.

3d

Telephone

That night, as the McIntyres were seated at the kitchen table eating their dinner, the telephone rang.

The telephone rarely rang in the McIntyre household but when it did it was invariably for Mr McIntyre. It was Mr McIntyre who normally answered the telephone and that Monday was no different. It was something quite out of the ordinary, though, when he re-entered the kitchen and said:

'Alice, it's for you.'

The expressions flowering over the faces of his wife and daughter suggested that this statement was puzzling enough without him uttering the significant addition:

'It's a *Graham Lironi.*'

The significance of the addition lay in the fact that the name of the caller revealed him to be a member of the *opposite sex*. The addition meant that Alice's puzzled demeanour – which intensified because, as far as she was aware, she did not *know* a Graham Lironi – was compounded by mortification.

Relieved to leave the kitchen table, she entered the living room and, with some trepidation, lifted the waiting receiver:

'H-H-H-H-H-Hello?'

'You okay?' asked the voice.

She recognised it immediately as the biker's.

3e

Secrets

They arranged to meet that Saturday. Alice spent the interim painting fantastical scenarios. When the day finally arrived she was a wreck of quivering trepidation.

This was partly because Saturday constituted her first-ever date. In the self-imposed confinement of her bedroom she had evolved a naive – since it was not born of experience – romantic conception of love. Love, she envisaged, would come and irrevocably change her circumstances.

She was ready for the change.

Was Graham Lironi the harbinger of love?

The trepidation was also partly because Saturday spawned her first-ever lie to her parents. This may have caused her some consternation but it was long overdue. That Saturday was significant for the birth of Alice's first-ever secret.

Secrets may be dangerous, but they are evidence of having something worth keeping to yourself.

3f

The Tunnel

Six months later the McIntyres were seated at the kitchen table eating their dinner when Alice cleared her throat and stammered:

'I-I'm p-p-p . . . p-p-p . . . pppppreg-nant.'

Her parents waited for her to deliver the punch line. When it looked as if it might not materialize, they stared at each other; their cutlery remaining absurdly poised in mid-air. Finally, as if emerging from a spell, Mrs McIntyre said:

'The . . . father?'

'G-G-Graham L-L-LLLironi,' replied Alice. Sensing their shock, she added, 'We're going to g-get mmm-ma-ma-ma-marr-ied.'

Later, in the consoling womb of her room, Alice reflected on the stark contrast in the reaction to the same item of information between her parents and her lover. While her parents had entered into a catatonic trance, Graham, who had admittedly blinked a moment in surprise, had taken her in his arms and birled her around in a deliriously dizzy moment of glory, the memory of which would rise like a bubble from her dark and distant past to burst open upon the surface of her present some sixteen and a half years later.

The grandfather clock struck nine times and then Alice heard three soft taps on her bedroom door. Bidding her visitor enter, she was surprised to see the strained visage of her father peering round the door frame. She could not recall him ever entering her bedroom before. She waited for him to reveal the reason behind this extraordinary visit. For his part, her father pulled nervously at the skin covering his Adam's apple.

Then he said:

'Your mother and I have been talking.'

He proceeded to address the foot of the bed upon which Alice reclined. He spoke of how he and his wife had devoted their lives to the upbringing of their daughter. He spoke of their quiet pride in her application to her school work, and even confessed that they found the expression of their love difficult. He spoke of his own, confused childhood and suggested that she had now reached a 'critical crossroads' in her own where it was vital that she choose the correct route. He told her that the choice of route was hers and hers alone.

She followed his train of thought as it chugged along its mundane track. His voice and his words had a soothing effect which lulled her into a sense of security. Then, unexpectedly, the train swerved into a tunnel. Mr McIntyre had made a suggestion to his daughter which utterly revolted her.

'Ggget *out!*' she screamed.

As soon as she could, she left home and settled in a town called East Kilbride.

3g

Twins

Alice gave birth to twins seven months later.

The brother was born one minute before his sister. Apart from their reproductive organs, the only distinguishing feature between the babies was their hair. The boy was blessed with a headful of glossy black, while his sister was pure blonde.

The girl was in fact an albino. As a child, her blonde cherubic features gave her an angelic quality. Alice enhanced this effect by dressing her newborn daughter in white and, by way of exaggeration, dressing her newborn son in black.

It was a habit which stuck.

When Carol and Carl were ten years old, Alice sat them down and told them of their father's death in a motorcycle accident a week prior to their birth.

4a

Solitude

Carl fled the Alps and returned to the equilibrium that was his homeland. But instead of acting upon his impulse, which was to confess to the murder of his own beloved sister, he reasoned that solitude would help him determine the course of action appropriate to his disturbing circumstances.

Because of this misty logic, Carl, upon his arrival in Glasgow, instead of rushing to East Kilbride, set off for Rowardennan to scale Ben Lomond. He camped on the summit for seven days and nights.

On the seventh night he had a dream.

On the eighth morning he left for home.

46

The Seventh Night

A flame of happiness ignited inside and a warm glow infused his whole; thawing arctic landscapes of torpor and rising up from toes through groin and intestine into heart and lungs and up, up until it threatened to scorch the cold fortress of his psyche.

The cause of this combustion was the idyll before his wondering eyes. He inhaled the fresh scent of banana, sea and sand and, emerging from a momentary reverie, took short, tentative steps across the burning rocks which separated him from his unforeseen discovery.

Soon the breadth of the horseshoe bay was laid bare before him. He stood with roasting soles, momentarily unable to step forward and corrupt the virgin cocaine-white granules of sand, transfixed by the aquamarine ocean lapping the shore, and belatedly realized he'd trodden on the perfect powder. Raising a sole to assess the damage done, he saw the sand's first footprint. A momentary lack of concentration had ended an infinity of perfect peace. The impression he left had become his signature.

This was now *his* territory.

He beheld the fascinating vista surrounding him: the

enticing cobalt lagoon; the emerald foliage dotted with splurges of buttercup bananas; the clay cliff from which, moments before, he had made his cautious descent; and he removed his clothing. He had passed through an intangible rite of passage and wished to pay tribute by destroying past paraphernalia. No longer would he soil his skin by furtively concealing it beneath artificial textiles.

He would live in the natural naked state.

The mother sea beckoned him back into her secure beginning. He responded to her welcome invitation to cleanse his skin from the filth of necessary trivia before it might penetrate deeper. It had been a long time since he had felt clean.

The sun sparkled on the surface of the sea, dazzling and dancing to the tune of nature. He dipped a toe into the water then submerged his aching feet. The only sound was ripples caressing the shore; a never-ending song without melody but constant rhythm in sync with his heartbeat. He had come upon his natural environment, *feeling* this as a truth rather than learning the knowledge.

He waded into the lagoon, basking in the seductive sensation of tonic water rising up dry, cracked skin and bone, licking leaden legs light and free. Swaying Hawaiian grass skirts tickled his underside while a ravine of scarlet coral dared him to poke. A shoal of tropical fish glided over a bed of perfectly white smooth egg-shaped pebbles. Sliding on an egg, he lost balance and submerged into the dumb wet world with a splash.

Regaining composure, he thrust his head above the surface and guzzled gallons of air, exulting in the notion that he was fresh and clean and new-born. Floating there on the water's ebb and flow, weightless limbs spreadeagled, he accepted the bland beauty of the unblemished blue sky.

His meditations were distracted by a lightning slither of silver darting underwater. He scrutinized the sea in taut suspense then swivelled round to find himself nose to snout with a dolphin.

Then, as suddenly as it had appeared, the dolphin vanished. He searched the water frantically and, at the moment when he began to doubt if it would return, was uplifted. The dolphin was underneath him, pushing him up out of the water, up on to its back, up into fresh air in a perfect parabola, and down to hit the water with an almighty splash.

Thus began a tempestuous merry dance above and below sea level, punctuated by practical leaps into the air prior to plunges to the sea-bed and, caught up in this voyage, Carl for the first time extracted the full satisfaction to be had from an activity *as it occurred*.

Then, too soon, the present turned to past. It was time for the dolphin to depart. By way of ingenious contortion, it walked backwards on the water, clapping flippers, giggling cheerfully.

Carl waved and the dolphin sank without trace. Wondering if they were destined to meet again, he sighed and swam back to shore. He dragged himself on to terra firma, light and refreshed, and lay propped on sinking elbows. Rollers broke on the beach sending shaving foam racing up the sand to cleanse his legs and splash his torso. Although he was looking out to sea, the messages his eyes sent to his brain were ignored by that grey receptacle due to its preoccupation with another subject entirely.

He was thinking about himself.

Then he realized that he was squinting because he was

being dazzled by a blaze of sunlight bobbing on the waves. He became intrigued by the waves playing pitch and toss with the bouncing ball of sun. His fascination won, he waited with delicious anticipation for the waves to deliver up this enigmatic object for examination. Soon the mystery would reveal itself, for there were the white horses galloping ashore, bearing the beacon, tossing it ahead to be swept up between his legs and spill its hissing black bile into his belly button, trickle down his torso and rape the virgin sand. The object was a tin can and it bore the familiar legend *Coca Cola*.

Disgusted, he scrambled to unsteady feet. Unconsciously, even though he watched himself, he crunched the vile container in his fist. The concrete world, he was thinking, was a spoilt brat shitting on the fruits of its Mother's labour with malevolent delight, wilfully destroying his blessed kingdom. He fled into the forest green.

He was in the heart of the lush jungle before he realized he still held the strangled object of his torment in the palm of his hand. Immediately, he loosened his grasp and let it fall, but he could not leave it there; it would poison the jungle. Loathingly, he lifted the can once more. How was he to dispose of it? There were no litter bins in paradise. He resigned himself to being laden with this relic from the dead grey place.

He proceeded through the camouflaged kingdom with trepidation. Parched and sweltering, he longed for water to quench his thirst and restore his sapped vigour. As if in answer to his prayer, struggling valiantly against the sound of brute creation, he heard the running of water. As he proceeded, the crescendo rose from a faint trickle to a raging torrent. The air grew lush and damp. Cracked lips welcomed moisture and beads of fresh water mingled with those of stale sweat on salty brow. Soon the forest came to an abrupt halt and there, before him, lay the source of the resonant roll.

He was standing on the edge of a steep cliff-face, his arms aloft to greet the breeze, transfixed by the sublime splendour ahead. Across a watery canyon, partially shrouded by a smooth blanket of cotton-condensation, lay the majestic spectacle of a waterfall. A cascade of foaming white water rushed down a sheer gully into the calm distant blue of a small ocean basin far below, while, above, a beautiful rainbow arched over the mouth of the Niagara.

Carl became aware of his reaching arms and self-consciously let them return to dangle by his side. It occurred to him that, had anyone been watching, they might have thought he was preparing to dive into the inlet. Amused by this notion, he raised arms aloft and rolled himself on to the balls of his feet in imitation of a diver. He stepped forward as close as he dared to the very edge of the cliff.

While the height instantly quelled any urge he might have had to try the dive, another part of his brain simultaneously perceived that there was a clear, sheer drop with no visible rocks beneath the surface of the smooth, sparkling turquoise.

He stepped back from the cliff-face.

Shielded from the up-draught, he became newly aware of The Token From Hell he held in his hand. Instinctively he corkscrewed his body and drew his arm back in preparation for launching Satan's symbol in a supreme act of catharsis when, at the final moment, his eyes perceived the panoramic beauty of the spectacle his haste would forever tarnish.

His fingers refused to loosen their stranglehold.

In another second he found himself sprinting at an arc away from the cliff-edge towards the rain forest and realized that the conclusion of this anti-clockwise motion would lead back to his starting position. But something in the mixture of frustration, fear, anger, excitement and desire to express contempt via a definitive act all boiling up his bowels had the paradoxical effect of leading him to accelerate the momentum and propel his body over the ledge.

Air gushed into his temporarily paralysed breathing apparatus and combined with the waterfall into a horrific white-noise wall, then suddenly it was all over with a brutal splash through to a deep, dark lull. Straining and stretching desperately for the surface, he thrust his torso through the water on the brink of bursting bellows, and laughed madly.

A loud splash distracted his attention. Before him, heartily applauding his jump, was the silver dolphin. Carl's immediate reaction was to ask if it had witnessed his leap, in the manner of a child desperately trying to win praise from a father shielded by a catalogue of current affairs.

No sooner had the dolphin appeared than it ducked beneath the waves again, resurfacing a moment later with the Coke can balanced precariously on the tip of its tail. A quick flick, and the can was spinning through the air to land back in Carl's palm.

Then he was treated to a second seafaring voyage as his host led him out of the turquoise basin and into the ocean. He strained his neck to steal a last glimpse of the rainbow waterfall, in the realization that in a moment it would become part of his past.

A breathtaking skim across wind-whipped, cream-topped waves around a Cape of Good Hope and he was deposited back in the bay. A pall of pale green smoke tumbled skywards from a blazing inferno. Ash debris floated down to drown sizzling on white horses. The dolphin ducked beneath the waves and disappeared, leaving Carl to unravel the mystery of this angry combustion alone.

He waded ashore, dragging lethargic limbs through the sea, clutching the Coke can in his fist. He had become bonded to it now. It was as if his hand had been created to cradle this tin can. They had shared many an experience, can and man, and his hatred for it had subsequently mellowed in relation to its elevation to talisman status.

The jungle shimmered behind the wall of flame. Through the waves of heat, the branches of a tree twitched unnaturally and a man strolled on to the beach. He was large, portly and middle-aged and he sucked at a bottle of beer. His thinning white hair, blue-white whale belly and the rivers of sweat running down the ravines of his red face betrayed him as a stranger to this land. His shorts, which stretched to contain his girth, were tartan. Removing the bottle from his lips, he dragged a paw across his mouth and belched loudly.

Then he noticed Carl.

Carl was standing at the water's edge, attempting to shield his exposed groin with the Coke can. The quandary of being caught naked stalled the engine of his body, rendering him immobile. Although his vexation was palpable, the stranger chose not to recognize it and, instead, resolved it by informing Carl that he had placed his clothes beside the fire.

In a reassuringly familiar burr, the man invited Carl to join him in a lunch of fish and beer. Wary, but to some extent emboldened, Carl accepted. It was not too long before the two had established their common nationality. This struck Carl as a remarkable coincidence but his fellow countryman simply shrugged and muttered something to the effect that all our lives are intertwined.

A silence developed between them, then:

'Why're you running away?'

The question took Carl by surprise:

'Pardon?'

'Why're you running away?'

Carl surmised that his guilt was transparent. 'Why should I run away?'

'I don't know. *You* tell *me*.'

'*I* don't know.'

Although they were alone and in no danger of being overheard, the man leaned forward and spoke in hushed, conspiratorial tones.

'There's no need to, y'know,' he said. '*I* know.'

'How?'

'It doesn't matter *how*. I just do.'

Carl shrugged and then the man asked:

'D'you believe in God?'

'No.'

'Pity,' sighed his adviser. 'Then listen to JC.'

'Pardon?'

'Listen to JC.'

'Jesus Christ?'

The man shook his head then pulled a face and said:

'Maybe – but I was thinking of Jiminy Cricket.'

'Pardon?'

'Give me your Coke can.'

Carl followed the man's line of vision down to his hand and discovered that, sure enough, he still held the can. Bewildered, he handed it over. The man thanked him and bent it back into shape. As he did so, he sang:

No matter how far you run
you can't escape JC.
No matter what you've done
You can't escape JC.

When he was satisfied that he had returned the can to its original shape, he turned it upside down. An object fell into the sand which he retrieved and tossed to Carl. It was a golden container the size and shape of a fuse.

'Open it,' said the man.

Carl did as he was bid. A tiny parchment was curled inside. Written there were the words:

Always let your conscience be your guide.

Carl rose and entered the jungle to relieve himself of the beer he'd consumed. There, in a shaded area, he pissed a great and golden arc. Returning to the shore, he noticed his host's vesture dangling from a branch of a tree and was intrigued by a ring of white glinting in the sunlight.

4c

Three Sources of Guilt

Carl remembered Carol and the circumstances of her death.

He blamed himself and was plagued by guilt. First, because it was he who had cut the rope which had plunged Carol into the abyss, and secondly because it was he who had manufactured the argument which caused Carol such grief and led to her blind panic and subsequent stumble over the cliff.

Carl had woken that fateful morning on the mountain with an acute sense of melancholia. Although he had scaled new peaks of joy the night before, he woke to find that he had plumbed equally deep troughs of despondency. The transformation in his temperament was inexplicable to him. It was also transparent that it had been inexplicable to Carol. This observation served only to compound his melancholy and deflect some of his self-loathing towards her.

It was then that Carol had said:

'Carl, be honest with me—'

And a cynical torrent had erupted from his mouth to the effect that honesty was a concept which had no instance in reality. It was this assertion which led to Carol's challenge and resulted, ultimately, in her death.

The root of his third strand of guilt lay in his false responses to Carol's challenge, which he had used to reinforce his eruption. *That* was his main mistake. Rather than consider the truth of his ejaculation, he had opted to play a game.

The game he chose to play was to respond falsely to the questions posed by Carol for the duration of her three-minute challenge. His intention was to have his responses accepted as truth and then expose them as false. The game was a means to an end. The end was to prove his earlier assertion that in reality honesty did not exist and for a moment he had swallowed the superficially attractive proposition that ends justify means.

He realized now that what he had done was to play God with Carol's emotions. He had known his answers would cause her grief. The grief was supposed to have been temporary. In the event it was permanent.

'Do you . . . love me?'

'I . . . don't know,' he had said. 'I don't know if I even *believe* in love. I'm not certain it exists.'

Although there could be no doubting the fact that Carol was dead, Carl doubted the fact that Carol was dead.

He remembered how his conscience had troubled him that morning; it had told him that he had committed a sin, but it had remained silent the night before. Or had it? Perhaps he had chosen not to listen? Perhaps his conscience had been deafened by love? In the morning, when the torrent of passion had subsided, had it not bawled its reprehension? If there is one thing that can deafen JC, he reflected, it is the lure of love.

Carl stopped and listened for JC. He waited, but heard nothing. Then, from somewhere, he heard a small, distant voice whisper:

'Where are you going?'

'I'm going home,' he said.

5a

The Cul-de-sac

Carl stood at the mouth of Avondale Place, the isolated cul-de-sac bounded by plantation that was the jungle of his everyday life. He had been standing there for some time. Though he had ventured from the cul-de-sac only days before, they had been stretched and straightened, like intestines freed from strict abdominal confines, into years. His eyes shone with the ghostly light of a man surveying the banal domain of a long-forgotten innocent youth.

Carol and Carl had spent the long bleak winter landscapes of their youth seeking an escape route from this suburban cul-de-sac. They lived in box number sixteen. Except for number seventeen's new-born, Carol and Carl were the sole representatives of the future generation. The middle-class middle-aged housewives must have loathed the pair as, oblivious to their stressful vigils behind twitching curtains, the twins screamed and shouted their juvenile joy into the spitting sky. NO BALL GAMES was the sign on the opal oasis. The plethora of golden nuggets of steaming canine excrement secreted amongst the blades of grass rendered the ugly scarred sign redundant.

He stood now upon the doormat before his front door. He

could not recall walking from the mouth of the cul-de-sac to his present position. Bewildered, he gazed back along the garden path to the gate which, moments before, he must have opened and closed and, with no recollection of having done so, fantasized that he'd stumbled through a trap door in time.

The reality was somewhat more mundane.

Carl's momentary lapse of memory could be more accurately explained as a consequence of his preoccupation with the terrible confession he was about to make to his mother.

The familiarity of the immediate vicinity which now confronted Carl struck him as odd. It seemed to him strange that the doormat upon which he now stood, the self-same doormat upon which he had stood almost every day of his life, should remain in the same position. It seemed to deny the events of the past days.

This sense of unreality was spectacularly compounded when the door before which he stood was yanked open not, as he had anticipated, by his mother, but by his twin sister.

5b

The Homecoming

Carol placed her hand beneath her brother's chin and shut his slackened jaw. Then she ascended the staircase, entered her bedroom and took care to close the door quietly but firmly behind her. She would not open it again till the following morning.

Still on the doormat, mouth agape once more, Carl was in a state of mystification when his mother, discovering her son standing in the doorway, rushed to greet him with a flourish of emotion. Alice McIntyre hugged him, kissed his forehead and pressed his head into her bosom. Such an open display of unbridled affection did little to diminish Carl's bewilderment.

You're h-h-*home!*' gasped his mother, stroking his hair. 'Y-You're s-s-*safe!*'

She led him through to the living room, ordered him to sit, and left to brew a pot of tea. It was only when her son had drained his cup that Alice, unable to contain her concerned curiosity a moment longer, requested that he disclose the nature of the Alpine incident.

'Did Carol not explain?'

Alice shook her head in agitation.

'Sh-She c-c-c-c-can't,' she stammered. 'Sh-She c-c-can't sp-sp-speak.'

'She's lost her voice?'

Alice nodded.

'So you've no idea what happened?'

Alice shook her head maniacally:

'Sh-she wr-wrote that y-*you*'d ex-p-p-plain.'

Carl sighed then recounted an edited version of the ill-fated expedition. His monologue began and ended with the words:

'I thought I'd killed her. I thought I'd killed my own sister.'

5c

An Opportunity

The leaves turned brown and fell from the trees before Carl was presented with an opportunity to reveal to Carol the torment which burned such a ghostly hole in his heart.

The opportunity had arisen late one Sunday afternoon when a weak sun had broken through the thick cloud of a morning's haunting shroud of cascading silver, the culmination of a weekend's heavy snowfall signalling the arrival of winter. Carl, acting on the bold advice of his mother, had invited Carol on an excursion to Calderglen Country Park, that oasis of nature within the asphalt secularity of East Kilbride. Much to his surprise, Carol had followed a shrug with a reluctant nod.

The nod had indeed been reluctant, for Carol had been instructed to accept her brother's invitation by the author of its contrivance. The months since Carl's homecoming had been an eternity in purgatory for Alice McIntyre as, helpless in dismay, she had observed the vacuum spread between her beloved son and daughter.

Because Alice had administered excessive doses of maternal medicine to no avail, she had arrived at the forlorn conclusion that the cause of the vacuum lay beyond her ken. She now recognized that the cure must lie within her offspring and that they alone were capable of its discovery.

Fearful of fate, Alice had deliberately avoided leaving her twins alone together these past months. Rather, she had sought to create a wholly artificial environment over which she might stand and observe like an omnipotent God. Admitting to herself the intrinsic artificiality of this manufactured kingdom, she concluded that she had no option but to risk allowing her children the chance to find their own cure.

5d

The Horseshoe Waterfall

They sauntered together down the steep gradient of a red cinder path leading to the Rotten Calder; together in the physical sense only. The silence between them had swollen to oppressive proportions. Carol had been struck dumb literally, Carl metaphorically. He used the silence to brood upon his stupidity.

After digestion of her son's version of the fall, Alice had related to Carl her explanation of its aftermath through the ingenious process of fusing the two tales, her son's and her daughter's, into one. The information Alice had been able to glean from her traumatized daughter had been ambiguous in content, imparting little by way of definition. Conclusions could be drawn only after the addition of Carl's guilt-ridden clarity and then the significance of Carol's strained attempts at communication had been revealed.

The most significant deduction made by Alice was that, rather than having fallen into an abyss, as Carl had assumed, Carol had fallen a substantially shorter distance; a distance so short that it had not posed a serious threat to her life. This deduction stunned Carl, though he was able to substantiate it through his recollection of the blinding blanket of mist.

He now berated himself for his gross stupidity in having leapt to the erroneous assumption that Carol's fall had been fatal. Why had he not sought to verify her condition? Alice was able to assuage his guilt over this detail to some extent with her reassurance that any attempt at verification would have proved futile, as Carol had been knocked unconscious by the fall. Alice had made this deduction from the rainbow bruise on her daughter's temple and Carol's own recollection of 'waking up' to a clear blue sky. The blueness of the sky was significant because, as Alice pointed out, it suggested that Carol had remained unconscious for hours rather than minutes.

Alice deduced that Carol, upon reawakening, made frantic by Carl's absence, and using the sun as her compass, had begun to weave a slow and tortuous route to the borderline. Carl's guilt heightened considerably when he learned from his mother that his sister, whom he'd left for dead, had sent out a search party for him.

They sauntered together down the steep gradient of the red cinder path leading to the Rotten Calder, the winter landscape an obvious echo of their last encounter with the pervading white wonder. By unspoken consent, they came to rest in the middle of a small wooden bridge spanning the Horseshoe Waterfall.

The river was in a hazardous condition. The Calder gushed over the waterfall's edge with bravado, cracking a thick window of ice into great shards before disappearing beneath the magnificent transparent barrier containing the surging torrent under its smooth glass lid with apparent calm. Long tapering spikes of ice dangled from the waterfall like gigantic jewels completing the glittering spectacle.

Carl spat into the face of the beautiful wall of water. Carol leaned heavily on the bridge, her head supported by her hands and her body weight centred on her bony elbows.

There was something in the air; the mutual recognition that they had reached a fork in the path of destiny which lay before them and the realization that if they were to make an informed choice between the alternative paths then some form of communication, whether it was to result in segregation or reconciliation, was inevitable.

Carl suspected, correctly, that the weight of responsibility for proceeding towards a cessation of hostilities rested with him. This mute war of attrition had, after all, erupted from *his* naive audacity to dare flirt with such potent forces as truth and love; but how to raise the white flag?

Then, in a moment of revelation, the memory of the ecstasy they had shared on the mountain top ejaculated like hot spermatozoa into the vagina of his enlightenment with such brute intensity that he was possessed with a pungent compulsion to express his truth:

'Carol?'

In studied contemplation of the waterfall, Carol made no indication that she had heard this prelude. Realizing the depth of her anguish, Carl sighed. Then he uttered three words of deceptive simplicity:

'I – love – you.'

Again there was no visible indication that Carol had heard this declaration. Carl attempted to articulate his emotions of the night on the mountain, explaining his bizarre behaviour that calamitous morning as a consequence of confusion and Pyrrhonism in reaction to her apparent resentment. In this he was speaking the truth. Carl *had* misinterpreted Carol's temperament that morning.

Yet still there was no visible indication that she had been

listening. He gripped her arms and swung her around. Again he whispered his declaration. This time Carol took his hand and pressed it to her abdomen. Carl remembered the gypsy's mysterious rhyme. He closed his eyes and embraced his sister as if his sanity depended upon never letting go. Carol, bewildered, wore a frown like a school uniform. The depth of her brother's emotion lay beyond doubt, but its nature remained a mystery.

When Carl opened his eyes he was confronted by a figure standing with arms akimbo at the far end of the bridge. The man was dressed in a billowing white smock smeared with a florid stew of tumescent war paint and a black beret dragged ludicrously low over his forehead. A Salvador Dali moustache twitched in the cramped cavity between his nostrils and lip, entirely incongruous beside the blunt sternness of his savage physiognomy. He chewed gum to the menacing beat of a war drum reverberating around the interior of his skull.

Carol, who had been facing the opposite direction, gasped into her brother's ear. Disembracing, Carl followed her startled gaze to the near side of the bridge where a figure in black blocked their retreat.

This second interloper studied the twins impassively, his ashen countenance a symbol of solemnity. He was clothed entirely in a deep funereal black, except for a stiff white dog collar which dazzled like a halo slipped from a place above his crown to choke his bulging throat. Carl recognized the sombre figure because this dog collar was the ring of white he had spied dangling from the branch of a tree.

Squeezing his sister's hand, he whispered:

'It's OK. I know him.'

A darting glance over his shoulders dispelled this display

of bravado. The man in the smock stood as solid as before, but he had advanced his position. The bizarre appearance of this improbable figure disconcerted the twins. There was something unconvincing about him. It was as if he had ineptly attempted to disguise himself as an artist but had succeeded only in the creation of an outrageous caricature.

Carol tightened her grasp on her brother's hand. Scanning her face, Carl was confronted by a self-portrait of panic. He ventured a smile of encouragement but it emerged as a grotesque grimace. Waving meekly, he greeted the rooted minister with a show of composure. But the minister betrayed not a flicker of recognition. Intimidated, Carl desperately sought to prompt his memory, but his frantic pleas crumbled before a wall of stolidity. Hysterically he swung round to see the man in the smock approach Carol. His sister suffered a paroxysm of horror, her defunct mouth contorted into a silent scream.

Carl was struck by a menacing thought. If the artist's attire was no more than a poor disguise, then could the minister's investiture too be a masquerade? The notion sent a jolt of petrification throughout his flesh. As if reading his thoughts, the minister yanked the constricting collar from his neck and hurled it into the gushing waterfall without removing his blank stare from the tragic twins who clung to each other and, like a pair of mesmerized spectators at a tennis tournament, switched to see the man in the smock fling his beret into the same aquatic fate.

With unflinching eyes fixed upon the pathetic pair, the intruders proceeded to reveal the extent of their terrorization. Ritualistically they stripped off their bizarre costumes to reveal flesh smeared with swathes of fresh crimson. As Carol vomited into the waterfall, Carl watched the man with the Dali moustache stab the air with a sparkling icicle lance. To his stricken sister he whispered words of vague reassurance. Then he approached the defrocked minister and began to babble:

'You told me about JC, remember? What's JC saying to you now? *Can you hear him?*'

His obsequious whimpering met with no mercy. The stolid wall remained solid. Grasping that he lacked the artillery to weaken it, Carl spun round to see the minister's bloodlusted accomplice raise the lethal spike of ice ready to plunge it deep into the heart of his prostrate beloved. His heroic lunge at the executioner was foiled by a mighty blow which sent him spinning straight through the wooden rail of the bridge.

He landed smack on his back on the river of ice. Gravely injured and barely conscious, Carl careened across this slippery hymen till it broke open to gulp him down into a perishing womb. Submerged in a stream of fathomless fantasy, he floated to the surface to discover that the vagina had closed over. In a frenzy, he pummelled the membrane through which he could perceive the blue of the sky.

Meanwhile, Carol's tormentor had tenderly placed upon her lips the sweetest kiss before ripping off his Dali moustache. Then he smiled, and Carol, recognizing him, fainted.

The minister knelt in prayer by the riverside.

Part II

THE GOSPEL OF THE SECOND CHANCE

Don't complain of your life.
There are no second chances.
That is the whole point.

Douglas Dunn

6a

Secret Negotiations

It was while serving sentence as a 'lifer' in a succession of Scottish prisons that James Nelson decided his future lay in the Kirk as a minister. When he first approached an official at the Kirk's offices in Edinburgh about entering the ministry, he was asked his reasons. The official was surprised when Nelson replied that he was in it for the money.

The Church subjected him to an intensive interview procedure after his release on parole in 1979 and he was given a place in the Faculty of Divinity at St Andrews University. After Nelson sat resits in some final year subjects for his Bachelor of Divinity degree, there followed secret negotiations with Kirk officials and a 'selection school'; an interview procedure used by the Kirk and the Civil Service to assess applicants where candidates are put through tests to determine their motives, and are interviewed by a psychologist.

Nelson was secretly accepted by the Church as an approved candidate four years before it was publicly revealed by Stewart Lamont and Murray Ritchie in the *Glasgow Herald* on 17 November 1983.

6b

The Great and Golden Arc

The first thing I did in this world was to piss a great and
golden arc. I've been pissing my life away ever since. Did
you know that piss was the original holy water?

I was born thirty-three years ago. Jesus Christ was cru-
cified at the age of thirty-three. My death will be less
melodramatic and a less significant event in the history
of mankind because the meandering beat of my haphazard
wanderlust pales in comparison with the straight path of
truth and love and faith trod by the Son of God.

Though the mediocrity of my beat is guaranteed, the
dream that one day I might stumble across that inspirational
path trod by Christ has, through the years, burned an eternal
flame at my core.

A volcano erupted at my core yesterday morning. Lava
trickled throughout my bowels. Flames scorched my tongue
and my meandering was at an end. My scatological beat had
assumed a pattern.

If I could trace my beat back to its source I'd discover a
single seed of introversion. It was from this seed that doubt
blossomed about what was and was not real. Until yesterday,
when lava cauterized its root, the fragrance of this toxic

flower slowly anaesthetized my essence.

My elder brother was also born thirty-three years ago; elder because he beat me in the race out of our mother's womb, thus winning the glory of first-born and the corresponding attention that title entails. I followed at his heel, content to wallow in his slipstream and sidestep the euphoria inherent in the birth of a new life, announcing my arrival with the great and golden arc while our mother, having delivered two new lives, lost her own.

As it was in the rush from the womb, so it was to be throughout our lives. Whereas the seed at the source of my beat is *in*troversion, the seed at the source of my brother's is *ex*troversion.

Because we are identical twins, this difference between *in* and *ex* assumed great significance. It was the creator of our individual identities, the means through which others were able to distinguish between us and the dominant factor in the decisions leading to our divergent destinies.

I was and am ambivalent about it.

I developed a theory that my brother's extroversion was a trophy for his triumph in the race from the womb, with my consolation being the right to follow at his heel throughout the remainder of our lives; a right of which I divested myself at the age of sixteen. An alternative hypothesis, developed much later, was that my brother's extroversion was inherited from our father, while my introversion was inherited from our mother.

Since my introduction to the world was to coincide almost exactly with my mother's premature departure from it, this hypothesis was never afforded the luxury of scientific test. Like many a sanguine scientist before me, though, I refused to permit this minor irritation to hinder the formulation of the terrific postulation clouding my perception. In time it became the steam which propelled my internal engine.

This accepted truth produced a secret bond between myself and my vision of the mother of whom fate had robbed me. While this bond took me closer to my unreal mother, it distanced me from my very real father.

I returned a verdict of guilty upon my father on the charge of apportioning the blame for the death of his lover – my mother – upon myself. It seemed to me that his resentment over her coincidental murder was to seep like a cancer throughout his decaying viscera. The medicine he prescribed to dull his desolation was whisky. The dosage soon escalated to an undiluted bottle a day.

The death of my mother and the birth of my brother and me signalled the second crisis in the life of my father.

6c

Brothers-in-Arms

His first crisis occurred in 1943.

During the Second World War a fifty-seven-strong group of Italian Alpine refugees presented itself in the Zermatt district of neutral Switzerland after a courageous Alpine escape from Champoluc in the Val d'Ayas over the Felikjoch.

My father was one of them.

He remained in Switzerland for the duration of the war. While there, he befriended a Scottish soldier who, as an escapee from an Italian prisoner-of-war camp, had forged a similar Alpine passage to peace. The two men shared more than their common crossing. In 1943 they were both twenty-one, with a thirst for adventure and whisky.

My father had ample opportunity to quench his thirst for the latter when he accepted an offer of work from the Scottish POW, whose family owned a Scotch whisky distillery in Auchtermuchty. Although he was to remain at the distillery for quarter of a century, working initially as an apprentice cooper and latterly as a master blender, for eight years he managed to resist the temptation to anoint his parched lips.

Shortly after his arrival in Scotland he suffered from an

illness which confined him to bed for two weeks. Five years later he married the district nurse who had replaced his fever with ardour. Three years of wedded bliss ended abruptly when his wife died in his arms immediately after bearing him twin sons. The conclusion of his temperance coincided with her death.

My father reared Gordon, my brother, christened after his benevolent brother-in-arms, and me with authoritarian devotion born of dedication to the provision of a standard of education of which he had been deprived. Although we were conscious of our peculiarity as a consequence of our homogeneity and maternal absence, Gordon and I grew up without any visible scars of trauma.

We learned the circumstances of our mother's death in the school playground at the age of ten. Until then our existence had been dualistic. A shell, protecting our peculiarity, had formed around us. The knowledge of the truth of our mother's death shattered this brittle husk and revealed the fundamental difference of the seeds at our individual cores.

The routine of our limited Ladybank childhood was marked by our attendance in the kirk of that suppressive village on each and every Sabbath. My father had inflicted this rigorous ritual upon himself with masochistic relish shortly after the death of my mother. For the first five years of our young lives, my brother and I were spared this Calvinistic indoctrination. It is possible that from my sixth year until my sixteenth, the three of us – my father, my brother and me – did not miss one solemn Sunday service.

This despite the fact that I had discovered my atheism on the night the circumstances of my mother's death were revealed to me.

6d

The Wheel

In my turmoil over her death, slumber had evaded me when I was stunned by a devastating realization.

I realized that in x number of years I would cease to exist. There was no denying the logic of this ascetic mathematic of mortality. All at once I had been sucked into the stark vacuum of a black hole; doomed to eternal purgatory.

In the morning I sought consolation in the postulation that, as I grew older, I would begin to understand and, perhaps, find a cure for, this anguish. I did not know then what I know now: that the growth process is more concerned with the dulling of, rather than the understanding of, anguish. Methods of dulling vary between those that are self-destructive and those that are self-distractive. An example of the former is to drown oneself in whisky, a method widespread throughout Scotland. Writing is a less prevalent example of the latter.

My anguish struck at irregular intervals, though always in the dead of night when dawn lay an infinity away. Beaten, my weary eyes followed the cruel clock crawl past, jeering at my impotence.

And the years shortened.

And I aged.

Because I lived beneath a strict routine bounded by the organization of education and religion, an image of the days of the week soon evolved within my mental sphere. Although my routine has since altered, and is now bound by the organization of occupation, this image has proved persistent.

The image is of a wheel divided into seven equal segments by its spokes, each segment representing a different day of the week, that is,

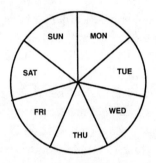

where one revolution of the wheel is equivalent to one week. Each day of the week is branded with its own indelible characteristic and is simply a repetition of itself: one week, that is, one revolution earlier.

It has recently come to my attention that the wheel is revolving faster. It is accelerating down a steep slope, leaving a faint trace in its track, fading fast, and the slope, of course, has an end.

6e

Clichés

That Sunday, as I manned my usual position in the pew – my father seated to my left, my brother to my right – the same old minister brought his worn sermon to an unconvincing conclusion and led his dwindling congregation into The Lord's Prayer. As always, I dutifully placed my clammy palms together, bowed my head and closed my eyes.

Then I did something which I had never dared do before.

I opened my left eye and checked that my father's were shut tight. Then I opened my right eye and verified that my brother's eyes too were closed in prayer. Emboldened, I raised my line of vision and gloated at the flock of gullible heads bowed in compliance at this altar of axiomatic acceptance surrounding me, when my eyes were singed by the burning glower of the sole witness to my unique act of profanity – the sinister minister. Hastily I clasped my hands, bowed my head, closed my eyes and obediently intoned *Amen!* with all the solemn sincerity I could muster at such short notice, with the rest of my fellow flock.

It's a cliché, I know, but that fledgling blasphemer seems today like a different person. But then clichés *are* clichés because their basis is in truth.

6f

The First Crisis

The first crisis in the life of myself and my brother, and the third in the life of my father, occurred when Gordon and I were sixteen and he was forty-five.

The inscrutable similitude of my brother and me reduced discrimination between us to speculation and presented us with endless opportunities for duplicitous exploitation of third parties. The temptation to indulge in such exploitation proved irresistible to Gordon and he acted upon it in many comedic episodes throughout our adolescence.

Although I was not immune to the temptation, my introversion helped me resist its power through the suspicion that, in addition to the production of comedy, here too was potential for tragedy. Subsequent events proved my suspicion to be justified.

My crisis was a consequence of my sole succumbing to the temptation.

By the age of sixteen, the seeds at the core of my brother and myself had sprouted to the extent that their inherent disparity had become externally manifest. While he had become the proud owner of a shiny back Norton, to which he devoted much of his time on those rare occasions when he was not actively relentless in pursuit of members of the opposite sex, I had become the proud owner of a shiny black Fender guitar, to which I devoted much of my time on those rare occasions when I was not fantasizing about actively pursuing members of the opposite sex.

It was a Saturday night at eight o'clock when Gordon's gang, as was its custom, screeched to a halt outside our garden gate and, fully aware of its effect on the residents of the street, blasted its horns. This clarion call was both an act of youthful rebellion deliberately designed to shatter the tranquillity of the night and a signal for Gordon to join them in the tantalizing exploration of the wonders of sundown. Distracted from my earnest strumming by the blasting of the horns, it was common for me to bid my brother a sardonic farewell with a *Don't do everything I wouldn't do!* as he leapt downstairs and sped into the dark.

But that particular Saturday night had been different because at eight o'clock Gordon had still to arrive home. Having spent a delirious day of discovery in the dunes of the west sands at St Andrews with a girl called Alison, he had been unavoidably delayed due to the fickle nature of the local public transportation network.

Therefore, at the customary eight o'clock blast of the horns, it was not Gordon who bounded out into the twilight — it was me.

I had succumbed to the temptation of exploitation. As I kick-started the engine, revved the throttle and spat on to the road with as much machismo as I could muster, I felt the thrill of duplicity and the delicious danger inherent in the possibility of imminent discovery.

In the event, although I suspected that some members of the gang, Dave D in particular, harboured suspicions about my identity, I was satisfied that I'd sustained my deception from the initial ride to the off-licence in Cupar, throughout the visit to the nearby hostelry and on to the subsequent gatecrashing of the party.

Including myself, the gang was five-strong. Besides myself, it comprised Johnny Sex, the noble acne-ridden leader, Dave D, a runny-nosed diminutive bifocalled misfit, and Pete and Paul Bird, brothers intent on stretching sibling rivalry to snapping point. Without exception we were clothed entirely in black leather.

We huddled conspiratorially around a table in a dark corner of a bar in Cupar. Our secluded symposium centred around the fact that we didn't 'give a fuck'. The expletive *fuck* appeared on at least one occasion in each utterance made by any gang member. In order not to appear conspicuous, I felt compelled to yield to peer pressure and adopt this uncouth custom.

The symposium furnished me with four fascinating facts about my brother. First, I discovered that his favoured brew was a vile concoction of lager and cider called snakebite. Second, that his nickname was Zola.[1] Third, he had first 'got his hole' at the tender age of thirteen one Saturday morning during his paper round when he was hauled into a hall and seduced by a woman while her husband lay

----

[1] The nickname 'Zola' derived not from the renowned French novelist, but from a blue-veined Italian cheese. It was an abbreviation of '*Gordon*zola' which was a distortion of 'Gor*gan*zola', the relevance being that it was Italian and so was Gordon's surname.

snoring in the bedroom upstairs. Although my naivety meant that I harboured substantial doubts about its authenticity, this third revelation sent sweet-scented scenarios of sex shooting through my senses which soon soured with the fourth revelation.

The fourth revelation I learned about Gordon was that his twin brother was a 'poof'. The dynamics of this were such that they necessitated a tactical retreat to the urinal where I licked my wounds while simultaneously cursing Gordon for his preposterous blasphemy and myself for my own conceit in daring to indulge in such dangerous deceit. Wallowing there in a lukewarm pool of tortured mental masturbation, I became intrigued by my reflection in the mirror and, after a moment's panic when I did not know whether I was myself or my brother, I determined to wreak revenge.

By the time we were snaking our way to the party, I was revelling in my adopted role of exaggerated extroversion. Yet, following our dramatic entrance into the tumultuous celebration, it was not long before I realized that, unless swift action were taken, exposure of my true identity was inevitable. This was because, while the black leather worn by my fellow gangsters seemed irresistible to a significant proportion of the opposite sex present in the room, a far greater proportion remained impervious to the charms of my own gear, resulting in a dearth of femininity in proximity to my person.

Recognizing the need for drastic action, I slipped quietly from the room while my comrades were distracted in the watering of their budding libidos.

As I ascended the stairs intent on my second tactical retreat to a urinal that night, I saw her. She stood at the stairhead, barring my way.

I was disturbed by *déjà vu*.

She was dressed in black. The starkness of her dress and her silence set her apart from the rest of her sex. Her wishing-well eyes, pleading for a prince to appear and make sense of the mechanics of the universe, placed her as a lost soul wandering aimlessly in a desert of her own creation.

I recognized the look. Her mien was a reflection of mine.

I was seized by an instinctive desire to shield her from the flames of chaos which threatened to engulf us, and to lead her to safety wrapped in a security blanket of order. She swayed unsteadily while her wishing-well eyes swallowed the discarded coins of my soul.

There was something about her. There was something familiar about her. There was something familiar about her which I was unable to identify. This plagued me for the remainder of the night.

While its elusiveness deprived me doubly of the therapeutic effects of peaceful slumber for the first half of the night, its transference into inspirational recognition deprived me likewise for the second. This transference occurred at the precise moment when I was able to identify her as the physical embodiment of my vision of my mother.

Then two guys barged past us and she lost her balance. I lifted her outside in the hope that fresh air would bring her around. Dabbing her simmering temples, I gloried in the notion that *I* was her saviour – as Gordon's gang formed a ring around us which no party animal, however curious, dared penetrate. When she regained consciousness I instructed her to hold on tightly as I kick-started the bike.

'Bye, Graham . . . I mean, *Gordon*,' called Johnny Sex, correcting a deliberate slip of the tongue.

7a

The First Summer

British Summer Time, which runs an hour ahead of Greenwich Mean Time, adds an hour of daylight on to an evening. While I welcomed this additional hour, winding my watch forward, only to readjust it once more some months later, was the source of some disorientation. I experienced a similar degree of disorientation this morning, sixteen years later, when I flew between time zones.

In reality summer does not begin when watches are wound forward but at that imprecise moment when a light breeze first permits particles of pollen to impregnate the air with the poetry of its fragrance of gold and the magical mix of heat and light settles down into our bosoms with a sigh of contentment.

The first summer I shared with Alice was also my last. The sun shone with such intensity that its rays radiate inside me even today. I understand this now, in retrospect. I have come to learn that it is easier to understand events in retrospect. More than that, the *only* possible means of understanding events is in retrospect. There is a cliché which says you don't know what you've got till it's gone and the basis of this cliché is also in truth.

It was the internal glow produced by this brief summer that helped me through the long winter of sixteen dark and cold years which, until yesterday morning, had shown no sign of drawing to a close.

From our first encounter, Alice monopolized my contemplations. This had a detrimental effect on my capacity for study. There was simply insufficient capacity for the concentrated application required for such mundane subjects as O-Grade Mathematics after the comprehensive meditation of Alice. What did the value of x and y matter in comparison with the bittersweet tang of her tongue?

My father disagreed with me on this.

As far as *he* was concerned, the correct calculation of x and y was of paramount importance. Inevitably, this difference of opinion led to conflict. After much heated debate I reluctantly accepted a compromise whereby it was agreed that I would confine my rendezvous with Alice to Friday and Saturday evenings and devote the remainder of the week to immersion in earnest study.

The cunning carrot designed to encourage my indulgence in this brief period of restraint and motivate my mental energies towards academic achievement was a protracted summer of freedom from paternal interference. In the event, it succeeded in the first of its objectives but failed in the second. While it proved sufficiently tempting for me to accept and abide by the terms of the agreement, the temptation proved insufficient for the mundanity of mathematics to conquer my intoxication with Alice.

The receipt of two items of information ended the summer with severe abruptness one sunny Wednesday in July. The first, received through the post and contained within a numbered brown envelope, was foreseeable. The second, received orally, was not.

The first item of information I received was the result of my O-Grade examinations. As I had anticipated, they were disappointing. I had failed Mathematics, Physics, Chemistry and French and scraped through English, Arithmetic and Art. My only 'A' was for Music. Gordon's envelope imparted the more welcome information that he had achieved eight straight 'A's. His reaction to his results was jubilation; mine was trepidation.

I dreaded my father's response to the news. In the event, he was to surprise me. After praising Gordon for his deserved success, he placed a hand upon my shoulder and consoled me.

The second surprise item of information which ended the summer was received that afternoon when I travelled to Cupar to meet Alice and, depending on her own results, congratulate or console her. In the event, congratulations were in order as she passed with the same monotonous consistency as Gordon.

Unusually, my mode of transport was Gordon's Norton. In a rare display of fraternity which, at the time, I suspected had been prompted by pity for my poor performance, but which I now suspect had been motivated by a burdening sense of guilt, he had offered its services to me for the afternoon. Alice and I chose to take full advantage of this unusual freedom and so embarked upon a journey to the seaside village of Lower Largo, to bask in the sunshine and paddle along the pebbled beach.

The news of my relative failure had put her in a quandary. Attempting to temper euphoria at her own success lest that seem selfish and smug, Alice sought not to console me too openly, lest that appear condescending. An awkward silence thus prevailed within which she endeavoured to express her mixed emotions through allusive winks and nudges. When all else had failed, she plumped for the risky, though urgent, humorous route to enlightenment.

It was while we were licking ice-cream cones and strolling past the statue of Alexander Selkirk, vaguely speculating on future prospects, that I unwittingly enquired about her hopes and aspirations.

Alice shrugged and deadpanned:

'As l-l-long as it has your l-l-looks and my b-b-brains, I don't really care what ssss-sex it is.'

7b

Gravity

There's a cartoon called Roadrunner in which a particularly speedy specimen of that swift species is hounded across the prairie by a wily coyote. The roadrunner, whose sole means of expression is the phrase *Beep Beep!*, is never caught. Instead, it constantly confounds its ravenous predator. On occasion it will lure the coyote over the edge of a cliff. At such times it is customary for the coyote to continue running, as though still on terra firma, until that moment when it realizes that there is no ground beneath it. After looking down, as if for confirmation, and seeing the ground thousands of feet below, the coyote will turn to us – the viewers – gulp, and wave goodbye. It is only then that gravity will take effect and the poor beast will plummet to earth, announcing its impact with a muted thud and a puff of white dust.

Like a coyote lured over a cliff-edge, I laughed appreciatively at Alice's remark and continued to lick my ice-cream. It was not until I caught a certain expression flickering across her face that I was able to discern my predicament – and then, like the coyote, I gulped.

I was still plummeting to earth when I honked my horn

and roared out of Cupar, having safely deposited Alice home a full hour earlier than what would normally have been considered necessary for me to meet Gordon's deadline for the return of his bike. The velocity of the descent was such that I was sent spinning into a state of mystification. Although I raced after it, the mysterious wisdom critical for comprehension lay teasingly beyond my grasp. Then, simultaneously, three things came together, heralding an explosion of volcanic dimensions:

1 I caught up with the mysterious wisdom
   and unravelled its mystery;
2 my metaphorical descent came
   to an abrupt conclusion following collision
   with a metaphorical ground; and
3 the motorbike collided, not metaphorically
   but literally, with a Citroën 2CV which had swerved
   around a corner on the wrong side of the road.

What happened next was entirely a consequence of the third of these simultaneous events. I became an involuntary projectile, hurled through the atmosphere in an acrobatic arc, coming to a rupturous rest in a raspberry field.

7c

The Sentinels

The disinfected fetor of bandaged decay infected my nostrils and awoke my sensibility. My renascent vision beheld the alien domain of a diabolic ward of white. At the foot of my bed stood two familiar sentinels bearing gifts of fruit and literature. With my skull wrapped tightly in gauze, my rib-cage imprisoned in a plaster-of-Paris cell and my right leg cast and hoisted aloft in a pulley, my armoured flesh felt foreign to me. It was the elder of the two sentinels who was the first to speak:

'How are you?'

I cleared my throat, pathetically, and croaked:

'Thirsty.'

He poured me a glass of water from a pitcher by my bedside. I drained it. Then he informed me that, following my recuperation, we were to relocate to Italy. After a moment's hesitation, I nodded. This same nod was returned by the first sentinel who then marched from the ward.

The second sentinel shuffled to my side and stooped to whisper in my ear. The visible degree of decay he had suffered since my slip into the void of coma disturbed me. His pallor pale, his eyes burdened by bloated black bags, he fidgeted and scratched his scalp.

'He was very concerned about you,' said the second sentinel of the first.

'I could tell.'

'When he heard, he went on a rampage of debauchery ending in his suspension from the distillery. He was discovered by Uncle Gordon's father teetering on a gantry railing while pissing a great and golden arc into one of those big copper stills.'

My eyebrows remained lowered, refusing to betray the extent of my agitation. The lack of any forthcoming visible or verbal response had a discomfiting effect upon the younger sentinel, who now shifted his weight and stretched to scratch a psychosomatic itch. Eventually he mustered the courage to broach the subject which lay at the source of his torment:

'You know about . . . '

I filled the pregnant pause with the same stiff nod I had exchanged with his elder. The motivation behind this timely interception was not compassion but self-preservation.

'I'm sorry,' he blurted. 'I know how much . . . it was never meant to . . . '

Unable to satisfactorily articulate his regret, he conceded defeat and hung his head. When he raised it again it was to ask my forgiveness. The pathos of this plea momentarily paralysed me. I could not, and so I did not, nod my head. Nor did I shake it. Gordon nodded his. Then he wished me a full and speedy recovery and bade me farewell.

He had just fallen into the same march from the ward as his father when he halted, spun round to confront me, and asked:

'Your accident . . . it *was* an accident . . . wasn't it?'

7d

The Injuries

It was in the heart of that long dark night that, as I lay awake in my hospital bed listening to the wretched whimper of my fellow invalids, I discovered the full extent of my injuries.

I had been walking through wonderland hand-in-hand with Alice when an urgent throbbing brought to my attention the fact that I had entered a state of tension. When I sought relief from this condition, I discovered the full extent of my injuries.

I could not feel my loins.

Appalled, I searched my nether regions frantically and was greatly relieved to find my manhood intact. While engaged in the relief of my tension, I realized that the source of my confusion lay in my other hand, which had been robbed of a sense of touch. I promptly fell into a long and deep sleep, reassuring myself that my numb hand was a temporary aberration.

When I awoke the following morning and bit the index finger of my left hand, I realized that my guitar-playing days were over. Although it remained physically possible for me to play the guitar, it would be impossible for me to play with feeling.

At noon Alice appeared by my side. An angelic vision of torment, she tended my martyrdom with the enlightened beauty of her smile and the balming brush of her wings. Softly she kissed my fevered forehead while her tender fingertips traced a melancholy melody along the lines of my palm. Then she seized my hand in her own and pulled it into the soft warmth of her breast.

At that moment I cleared my throat and announced:

'I don't feel anything.'

Her head jerked up to reveal eyes brimming in a broth of love and sorrow and mystification.

'Wh-wh-what d-d-do you m-m-mmmmean?'

Without hesitation I said:

'I mean I don't love you,' as callously as I could.

8a

The Exile

Why did God invent women?
Because sheep can't cook.

Why did He give them legs?
So they could walk from the bedroom to the kitchen.

Those revealing jokes were related to me in Scotland by a male native. They might just as easily have been related to me in Italy by a male Italian.

Where a common cultural characteristic exists between two nations, the appeal of mordant wit transcends barriers, be they national, geographical or vocal. Like clichés, the basis of jokes is in truth; admittedly, the humour resides in its distortion, but if there were no element of truth in the above jokes to begin with, they would not *be* jokes.

In addition to male chauvinism, there are at least two other common cultural characteristics shared by Scotland and Italy. The first is football and the second is religion. While team colours and denominations differ between nations, the passion each arouses in the heart of its natives does not. Yet all the evidence suggests that the proportion of passion present in the heart of the representative Italian is greater than that of his Scottish counterpart.

Over the years I have developed three theories for this phenomenon. These strive to explain the different proportions of passion present in the heart of the representative Scot and Italian through the consideration of *un*common cultural characteristics, and they can be divided into genealogical, meteorological, and dietary. They propose that the different proportions of passion can be explained by:

1 differences between Latin and Celtic traits;
2 differences between hours of sunshine and
   inches of rainfall grossed; and
3 differences between the grape and the grain.

My inclination is to favour the second theory because it suggests the attractive proposition that the *latent* level of passion present in the heart of the representative Scot and Italian is equal, with the commonly noted apparent difference being a consequence of the Mediterranean sunshine raising the temperature of Italian passion and the Atlantic downpour diluting the passion of the Scot.

As the product of an Italian father and a Scottish mother who spent the first half of his existence in Scotland and the second half in Italy, I am in the perfect position to comment on the common cultural characteristics of both nations. This is not to imply that I conform to the characteristics identified. I conform to none of them. I am an exile from both cultures.

8b

The Trinity

The tense trinity that was my father, my brother and myself can best be described in analogical terms. At its best, each of its three tangential elements could be represented as the line of an equilateral triangle, that is,

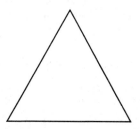

the attainment of an equilibrium where the forces of fate pulling us apart were exactly equal and opposite to the forces of destiny pushing us together.

As with most equilibriums, this harmonious triangularity was rarely, if ever, achieved. A more common structure of our trinity might have been better illustrated as,

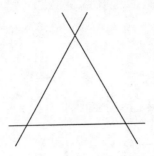

where each line of the equilateral triangle intersects the other, trespassing on the territory of its duplicates, unwittingly trampling hidden fields of dreams as a consequence of the forces of fate pulling us apart being less than the forces of destiny pushing us together.

When we arrived in the Alpine village of Champoluc in the Val d'Ayas precisely one week after my discharge from the flaking Victorian hospital ward, the trinity might have been shown as,

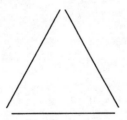

that is, the forces of fate pulling us apart were greater than the forces of destiny pushing us together with the result that each of us was left to float in a limbo with no clearly defined frame of reference.

It was during this period of cataclysm that my father

fought his final battle against the demon which intoxicated him, and my brother underwent a sensational conversion which culminated in his acceptance into the Catholic Church.

The move to Champoluc did nothing to slow the steady deterioration in Gordon's physical and mental condition. His stoop had become more pronounced, his fidgeting more manic and his moods more extreme and erratic. As the sun rose one morning, shortly after our arrival in the village, my father and I were woken from our slumber by an almighty *Hallelujah!* and confronted by a possessed Gordon proclaiming his new-found faith with preternatural fervour.

He disappeared that afternoon. I did not see him again until this very morning.

Gordon's sudden departure had an unforeseen effect upon the already strained relationship which existed between my father and myself. The removal of one line of the triangle meant that the remaining filial kinship was left without structure. The tenuous link between generations had been reduced to two lines floating randomly in divergent directions. Graphically, this might be illustrated as,

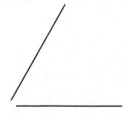

The looseness of this arrangement rendered calculation

of the relative values of the forces of fate to the forces of destiny meaningless.

Gordon's sudden departure signalled the start of my long and lonely path towards redemption. The method I chose to cleanse my sullied soul was utter dedication to the achievement of the same set of results which Alice and Gordon had gained a year earlier. The delayed glory from passing these and the following year's examinations presented me with a pleasant dilemma. I had applied for two different courses at the University of Bologna and now I had to choose between them. This was a difficult task. Through his attempt to influence my choice, my father succeeded only in complicating my decision-making process by kindling within me a desire for rebellion. It's only now, in retrospect, that I understand that the eventual resolution of my dilemma related back to Alice.

The appeal of the archaeology course lay in the unravelling of past mysteries as a means to a greater understanding of the present. The logic of such a method was not difficult for me to comprehend. The appeal of the economics course lay in the examination of the real mechanics of the present to the virtual exclusion of such unrealized notions as love and faith; notions which I had learned to distrust.

In the end I chose economics, which met with paternal approval. The decision was made instinctively, following the chance discovery of an item of trivia which startled and then intrigued me.

It is only now that I understand why.

What I discovered was that the father of economics was a Scot called Adam Smith who was born in Kirkcaldy. This link with my past life in Fife served also as a link with Alice. It was a link which I nurtured secretly until this very day.

8c

Abstraction

The model of perfect competition is based on the following assumptions:

- a large number of buyers and sellers;
- product homogeneity;
- free entry and exit of firms;
- profit maximization;
- no government regulations;
- perfect mobility of factors of production; and
- perfect knowledge.

Like every other economic model, it is an abstraction from reality. Such abstraction, economists argue, is necessary because the real economic world is too complex to facilitate meaningful analysis. Economic models, therefore, do not attempt to describe the *true* economic world because they are themselves *abstractions* from the truth. Abstraction, economists argue, does not necessarily imply unrealism, but rather provides a simplification of reality. That, *I* would argue, depends on the extent of abstraction.

Although I present lectures on such economic models

each day of my working life, I must confess to regarding them as spurious. I regard them as spurious because there is no way of measuring their validity. There is no way of measuring their validity because the extent of abstraction is an unknown quantity. The extent of abstraction is an unknown quantity because the economic reality is an unknown quantity. The economic reality is an unknown quantity because, economists argue, it is too complex to facilitate meaningful analysis.

Consequently, I have no faith in the gospel I preach.

There is a certain irony in my secret belief that if economics as a social science is to make any real progress then it must first be examined in the context of the real world. The irony is that my introduction to economics coincided with my own departure from the real world.

The second half of my life to date has become increasingly hermetic with each passing year. The slow slip into abstraction from reality started from the moment I waved farewell to the diminishing figure of my father on the platform and settled down to while away the journey to my rented accommodation in Bologna simultaneously immersed in the pages of a novel and the secret sounds emanating from my personal hi-fi. Such methods of passing time continued long after the train journey had disappeared down an interminable tunnel in my memory.

Partly because of devotion to my studies and partly because of the seed of introversion at my core, fresh friendships failed to flourish in Bologna. Songs and stories filled the empty space, not that there was much of that for me. My accommodation was a solitary cell with barely room for a single bed and desk.

I served a five-year sentence.

This masochistic period of detention comprised a punishing schedule of protracted study punctuated by short bursts of rest and recreation when I would seize the opportunity to lay down leaden books of incorporeal fact and lift revelational books of incorporeal fiction, diving still deeper into the well of abstraction.

It was during this period that I discovered the power of art – when I overheard the first of two songs which installed an element of identity into the abstract. It was called 'Candy Says' and it was performed by The Velvet Underground. It was the eve of my first examination at the end of my first year at university. I had spent the evening locked in my cell, poring over a plethora of painfully planned papers in a desperate final bid to prepare for my trial in the morning. When I had satisfied myself that I could retain not a morsel more of relevant information, I fell into bed, switching off the bedside lamp with one hand and switching on my treasured radio with the other.

After a moment of silence, 'Candy Says' floated over the airwaves and I lay motionless in the dark as a fragile beauty massaged my aching temples.

I discovered the second song only last year. On the last day of term, one of my students presented me with a gift; a record by a band called Aztec Camera. 'Just Like Gold' became the second song to distil my essence into its purest form and pour itself into me.

The enchantment of these two songs nourished a sensation of enlightened nostalgia. Both brought loss bubbling up from the depths to the surface of my consciousness. I myself had lost the opportunity to produce such inspirational works because I had lost the sense of touch in my hand. I had lost my one true love because I had lost the sense of truth in my heart.

I was confronted with the truth yesterday morning.

Preoccupied with the preparation of lecture notes, I glanced at my watch, only to discover I was late. Flustered, I rushed into the corridor and collided with an albino girl who handed me a card with the question *Mr Lironi?* written on it.

Intrigued, I nodded.

The second card she showed me read:

I am dumb.

The third:

I am your daughter.

8d

The Extract

Through a protracted and laborious series of cards and sign language, I learned of Carol and Carl's ill-fated homage to their unknown grandfather that was the Alpine crossing and the bizarre circumstance of Carl's death the day before yesterday. In between I learned of Alice.

I observed and, as the information percolated into me, recalled the lick of the flames from the fire which I had so cruelly sought to extinguish all those years ago but whose glowing embers still scorch my guilty bowels to this day. When Carol finished her tale, I felt the flickering flame stoke my soul and rise like a phoenix from the ashes inside me.

I learned that, until yesterday, Carol had thought I was dead. She discovered the truth when Alice had effected a reconciliation with her parents by inviting them to the memorial service for the grandson they had never known, and her grandmother had seized the opportunity to tell her about me.

Carol had decided there and then to find me.

'Why?' I asked.

Carl's memorial service is tomorrow, she wrote.

I side-stepped the need to respond to this information by canalising our communication on to the subject of Alice – then, just as suddenly, I fell mute and watched while Carol wrote of her mother. It was not long before she grew wise to my manoeuvrings. Mid-sentence, she stopped and scribbled:

You still think of her.

I shrugged.

Then you must come, she wrote.

I enquired whether Alice was aware of Çarol's whereabouts. This was an indirect approach designed to discern if Alice was the architect of her daughter's missionary zeal.

Carol shook her head.

I believed her. I had no reason not to. 'Past deeds cannot be undone,' I sighed. 'I cannot return.'

Each of us has a second chance, she wrote.

I said:

'Second chances do not exist in reality.'

Reality is determined by faith, wrote Carol.

She handed me an article torn from the front page of that morning's *Glasgow Herald*. A ringed passage enclosed quotes from a speech made by the Very Reverend Dr James Matheson during the General Assembly of the Church of Scotland debate which resulted in the acceptance of James Nelson into the presbytery. Carol had underscored the following sentence:

When we trust in Him our past is written off
and we are set at liberty for the future
which God has planned.

'But I am faithless,' I said, returning the extract.

She wrote:

Then you are dead.

That evening Carol boarded a plane to Glasgow and I boarded a train to Rome.

8e

The Confession

There's something awe-inspiring about standing at the entrance to a cathedral. This reverence is a consequence of the combination of an unknown quantity of factors and is akin to the sublimity experienced when standing at the top of a mountain. Cathedrals and mountains share the potential to raise awareness of the transient nature of existence. Silence plays a crucial role in both instances.

It was the first time I had ever been inside the belly of a cathedral. It was the first time I had been inside *any* place of worship for sixteen and a half years. Awed by the ceremonial ornamentation, I wavered by the font and distractedly dipped my numb hand into the holy water to sprinkle my brow.

The reverential ambience was made more palpable by the emptiness of the cathedral. I found myself wandering down the aisle towards the altar, regarding the enigmatic iconography, coming to a halt beneath a stained-glass window, where I stood entranced by the spectrum of its craftsmanship. When at last I turned away, my eyes fell upon a small plain black stall, secreted within the shadows of an enclave, the dark austerity of which, although in stark contrast to the enlightened beauty of the stained-glass masterpiece, intrigued me no less.

Strangely drawn to this black magic box, I found myself seized by a compulsive temptation to unravel its mystery. Upon entering the confessional I was branded a claustrophobic intruder by an oppressive powdery mildew. The abrupt shunt of a shutter startled me. Blinking, I was soon able to discern the silhouette of a figure beyond the grille. I brought the pregnant pause to a conclusion with what I prayed was the admission appropriate to such a circumstance. I said:

'Forgive me, Father, for I have sinned.'

'When was your last confession?' The voice, a queer helium high, seemed to parody sincerity.

'I've never confessed.'

'What is your confession?'

I sighed heavily:

'I've damned myself, and those I've loved, through a failure to forgive.' Testament to the truth of this tragedy was the fact that I was instantly recognized:

'Graham? *Is that you?*'

Stepping from the stall, I was mortified by the shadowy figure which met me. He nodded in recognition and I responded in kind. Conspiratorially I told him Carol's story.

'Why are you telling me this?' he asked.

'Carl's memorial service is today.'

He asked if I still loved Alice.

I shrugged.

'Then you must go,' he said.

I pondered this a moment. 'Carol says that each of us has a second chance.'

'Carol is wise.'

I shrugged. 'You know that *I* forgive *you*, don't you?'

He averted his eyes.

'Do you accept my forgiveness?'

After an interminable hesitation he shook his head violently.

'You're too late,' he hissed, lifting his vesture, revealing swollen ankles then bruised shins as I stood, a mesmerized observer until, suddenly, he yanked his robes above his waist and bared his eunuch identity.

I ran from the cathedral to the sound of my brother's cackle reverberating around his asylum and inside my head.

9a

The Echo

In the exceptional circumstance where doubt exists about the exact existential status of the loved one, perhaps because the whereabouts of his or her flesh and blood remains mysterious, speculation will often make its presence felt at some point during the occasion of a memorial service. Because Carl's body had yet to be found, his memorial service was just such an exceptional occasion.

Because Carl's body had yet to be found, he was presumed dead. From an emotional distance such a presumption seemed plausible, but the emotional limbo populated by Alice and Carol meant a glowing atom of hope that Carl had somehow survived would forever radiate within their hearts till irrefutable evidence – that is, the production of his corpse – would convince them otherwise.

Since such speculation is contagious, it was not long before the whole congregation had wandered into that limbo. Because I had been saturated in just this state for half my existence, the generic spirit was familiar to me.

The minister was engrossed in the verbose articulation of his summing speculations as I took my seat in the back row and scanned the congregation until I spied Alice. The rear of her crown became the oblivious recipient of my scrutiny for the remainder of the ceremony.

I did not know if I loved her. I did not know if I did not love her. I did not know if I had ever loved her. I did not know if I had ever not loved her. I did not know if I would always love her. I did not know if I would ever love her. I did not know if I would never love her. I did not know if she loved me. I did not know if she did not love me. I did not know if she had ever loved me. I did not know if she had ever not loved me. I did not know if she would always love me. I did not know if she would ever love me. I did not know if she would never love me.

But soon I would look into her eyes and discern that knowledge, like reality, is determined by faith.

The proceedings having finally drawn to an inconclusive conclusion, the congregation trickled into a dreich dusk while I, rapt in Alice, remained seated. I followed each faltering step of her passage down the aisle, brimming with anticipation of the moment when our eyes would meet for the first time in sixteen and a half years. Our eyes did meet as she passed by, but hers betrayed not a flicker of recognition. I followed her slow passage to the doorway, where, framed against a now blazing sky, she paused, as if lacking the strength or will to cross this final threshold, and swooned.

I rushed to break her fall.

As I write this sentence, later that same evening, I recall that, as I caught her in my arms, I thought I heard a distant echo of our first encounter.

10a

The Ordination

The Rev. James Nelson was ordained and inducted a Church of Scotland minister in Chapelhall church in Lanarkshire on 3 April 1986, becoming the first convicted murderer to enter the clergy of any Christian denomination.

When, in 1983, the *Glasgow Herald* reporters asked Nelson about the murder of his mother, he said:

'I am still surprised at what happened. I ask myself, "Did this really happen?"'

106

The Letter

I beseech you, in the bowels of Christ:
Think it possible you may be mistaken.

> *Oliver Cromwell*
> *Letter to the General Assembly*
> *Of the Church of Scotland*
> *3 August 1650*